Snow

Reflections

Believe that wishes are delicious & dreams do come true!

Katie White

Katie White Copyright © 2011

ISBN: 1461166470

ISBN-13: 978-1461166474

Cover art by Katie White 2011

This book is dedicated with love to my husband, Jeremy, who has remained by my side whether I was playing the heroine or villain of my own story.

CONTENTS

Author's note: It is the reader's own choice which tale to read first. Romantics may be more satisfied beginning with the Queen.

The Queen

I'd like to thank the talented women whose lyrics and/or vocals inspired the naming of each chapter.

Prologue: A Mother's Memory

The balance of life and death is more delicate than I could have imagined.   I saw the crystal flakes falling to the ground.   I heard the ravens flying by distressed by the sudden frost.   I felt the rush of warm blood leaving my body.   And as I gazed out the window at the virgin snowfall, I saw her in my mind's eye - my daughter!   Not the baby whose soul would be replacing mine in this world, but the woman she would one day become.   I saw the beauty of her fair skin, dark hair and red lips; I heard her sweet voice; I smelled the flowers she would gather in the forest; I felt the love she possessed in her heart.   Didn't I?   Or was I full of tender delusion?   In the end, her will to live exceeded my own.   Rightfully so, this story belongs to her and not me.

Nobody's Daughter

"Down at the bottom of the ocean I lay down,

Nobody's coming, just continue to drown."

-Courtney Love

I have no right to complain. There are people within my own kingdom who have suffered hardships I could never comprehend - poverty, sickness, grief, homelessness, the list goes on and on. My childhood was unhappy; to state otherwise would not be the truth. But still, I was raised a princess. I lived a privileged life. To feel such misery given the circumstances does not make sense. Loneliness is the name of the demon that gnaws at my heart. To an outside observer this would seem absurd, if not impossible. I live in a palace full of servants to attend to my every need. How can one be alone in the midst of so much activity, so many people? In truth, I feel that the very presence of all these people makes my solitude feel even deeper.

I have a connection to no one. No friends. No family. Not one person.

I never knew my mother. She died following my birth. The word "mother" holds so much wonder to me. In my ideal fantasies, I imagine who she was, and who she could have been to me.   I picture her combing my hair and tying my laces as the two of us laugh at trivial things that somehow seem enormously important.   If I stay in this reverie long enough, I can feel her arms wrapped around me in a loving embrace.

But eventually, I open my eyes and the fantasy comes to an abrupt end.   Then my heart grows dark, and I begin to hate her for leaving me. And then I hate me for killing her.   And I wonder why my unhappy existence is more vital than her life?   I decide that it is not and begin to wish that I was the one who had died instead.   And I sit and sit, hating us both.

The only reason I understand that joy is possible is because of my father.   He was my everything.   He doted on me as if I was the most important person in all the world.   Dresses of the finest silk were made to fit my small frame, books from foreign countries lined my library shelves, the most delicious pastries were created for my breakfast, and every Sunday, after spending the day in quiet prayer, a new porcelain doll would appear on my bed making me convinced that God answered my every wish. As I grew older, I realized that it was my father who made these things possible, and he was indeed Godlike to me.   Life was happy, but I took it all for granted; without experiencing misery, you can never fully understand joy.   I had no idea how quickly things were about to change.

A month before my seventh birthday, my father brought home a new bride.   I was so excited!   Anything that made my father happy, instantly made me happy.   Finally, I thought, I would get my longed for mother.

Then I met her and immediately realized I had been wrong; she would never be a mother to me. I felt no warmth from her, no love, no acceptance. In fact, I felt nothing at all, as if in her eyes, I did not even exist. The more my stepmother ignored me, the more I longed to please her, but it was a battle I could not win.

For my father's sake, I pretended that all was well, that we were one happy family. But in truth, my world was unraveling. My stepmother was demanding of my father's time and attention, and soon I saw him less and less often. Before long, I was eating porridge for breakfast and there were no longer new dolls on Sundays. The light in my life was growing smaller and dimmer until the day it was extinguished completely.

I remember it well because I awoke to blood on my sheets that morning. My head felt dizzy and my stomach cramped as a sickness I'd never felt before washed over me. Still, I had no idea I would be ushered into adulthood in more ways than one that day.

My father had been ill for nearly a week, and by my stepmother's command, I wasn't allowed in his bedchambers. I would have no "goodbye"; she would take that away from me as well. I heard the servants whispering about what a pity it was that the King did not die a heroic death defending his kingdom, but died from nothing more than a virus. Both of my parents were weak in body, and I pondered if this meant that I would be also.

Plans were simultaneously being made for the funeral procession as well as my stepmother's coronation as Queen. The next several days were a whirlwind of events that I was obligated to attend.   Inside, I felt completely numb, unable to process what was actually taking place.   I have scattered memories of those days, but am ashamed to admit that I remember nothing of importance.   I wish I could recall if my stepmother appeared sorrowful at my father's passing or satisfied that she had gained so much power as Queen, but I truly don't know.   Instead I remember the ugly dress I was made to wear to my father's funeral that had a frilly bow that seemed too silly for the occasion.   I tried to protest wearing such a garment, but was told that my stepmother insisted I wear this particular dress.   I couldn't imagine why she cared and wondered if the servants were making this up simply to avoid finding me another outfit.   But I was obedient and wore the hideous dress, noticing how uncomfortable it was throughout the funeral mass.   In retrospect, I'm horrified that I was distracted by something so insignificant, but I also know that if I had not been otherwise focused, the reality of the situation would have caused a nervous breakdown.

After the burial, I retreated to my room and told one of the servants that I was thirsty.   She returned with a mug of warm cider instead of the pitcher of water I was expecting.   It was not a chilly day, and I just stared at the beverage confused as to why it was brought to me.   I took a sip, and it was more sour than sweet.   In that moment, I finally broke down crying, overwhelmed with grief.   For some reason, that bitter apple taste represented how nothing in the world made sense to me anymore.

And once I broke down in tears, it was impossible to stop.   I thought for sure that my sobbing would never cease.   The pain in my heart felt like a bottomless abyss.   If one could truly die of a broken heart, I would've died a thousand deaths that day.   I was inconsolable for the next several months, not that anyone paid any attention to me.   The servants were entirely preoccupied making changes throughout the palace according to my stepmother's likes and dislikes.   The Queen was so intimidating that her orders were met with prompt response.   Everyone was so fearful of displeasing her that no one noticed the state of their Princess.   That's when it began.   Emptiness.   I felt nothing inside myself anymore.   When I looked in my full length dressing mirror, I saw myself as an empty shell with nothing inside.   My physical body remained whole, but within I felt numb.   Everyday the loneliness became more and more apparent to myself, but I hid it well.

I would not give the Queen the elation of seeing me unhappy.   So, I began to perfect playing the role of the sweet Princess just like an actress in a play.   The better I got at it, the more annoyed she became.   And thus, the years passed.   Instead of finding solace in each other's company, we each found moments of smug satisfaction in irritating one another.   Yet all the while, I hid behind external appearances as my self loathing grew exponentially.

Foolish Games

"These foolish games are tearing me apart,

Your thoughtless words are breaking my heart."   -Jewel

As the years passed by, there was no relationship to deteriorate between the Queen and me.   We were simply two women leading separate lives under the same large roof.   I was no longer a little girl, but not yet an adult confident enough to make my own choices.

If the Queen summoned me, it never occurred to me to refuse.   If she ordered me to go into the woods with the servants and gather berries for the cooks to make pies, I obeyed.   If she told me to wear a pair of dainty boots that pinched my feet, I did it.   For the most part, we largely ignored one another.   But on the rare occasions that we did speak, it seemed to be for the sole purpose of her to annoy me.

Not that I didn't do my best to irritate her right back.   No matter how condescending her requests, I always smiled and acted eager to comply.   I wanted her to know that she could not break me down.   I was sure she wanted to make me angry or sad, and I would not give her that pleasure.

In retrospect, I realize that if I had been more mature and could have approached her with honesty instead of an insincere grin, it might have helped to resolve our differences.   It was clear that she didn't see me as a real person, but in fairness, I did not see her as one either.

The Queen was stripping me of my power.   I was not aware, that as the Princess, I had a voice of my own in matters as well.   My body had transformed into that of a young woman, but my mind was still that of an intimidated child.

With so little self esteem, I guess it's not surprising that I acted as I did in those days.   I dressed in clothes more suitable for an attendant than royalty.   I didn't always wear shoes when walking in the garden. Sometimes I put my hair up with a ribbon to keep it out of my face. Occasionally, I would take a drink straight from the well in the middle of the courtyard.   It never occurred to me that a Princess should not behave in such a manner.

One day, as I was drawing water from a bucket in the well, I got lost in thought and began to daydream that it was a magical wishing well.   I imagined that if you told the well your deepest wish and it echoed it back to you, your wish would come true.   I looked around and there was no one in sight except some doves in the nearby branches.   I leaned over the well and got dizzy staring into its dark depths.   "I'm wishing..." I found myself saying.   Then I heard the well speak my voice back, "wishing...wishing..." And then there was nothing but silence.   What did I wish?   My life was without direction, and I didn't know how best to change my situation.   I'd grown cynical and no longer believed in the dreams I had while my father was still alive.   I was certain my dreams were not meant to come true.

Still, I hoped beyond all hope that someone out there might understand me someday. So, I half whispered, half pleaded with the well, "I'm wishing that I won't always be alone."

I expected the well to reply the cold hard truth, "alone...alone...", but instead I heard a masculine voice behind me say, "Granted." I was so in shock that I nearly fell into the well, but the young man grabbed me just in time and pulled me into his arms. It was then that I noticed how undeniably handsome he was and my heart began to race with embarrassed panic. "Sorry, I didn't mean to frighten you, " he quickly apologized.

"No, it's not your fault that I'm so clumsy," I said, admitting to my own foolishness.

"I wasn't trying to eavesdrop," said he, as if he were the one humiliated. Then he flashed me a smile of perfect teeth, and I was instantly mesmerized. "Would you like to take a walk with me?" he offered as if there were any possible way for me to turn him down.

"Indeed," I replied as I lead him to the castle rose garden. At first I couldn't help but stare at his dark, wavy hair, deep brown eyes, noble chin and heartwarming smile. I'd never seen so much perfection on one face! Then when I realized I was gawking, I tried to make polite conversation to mask how inferior I felt by his side.

"So, you must be a visitor at the castle?" I guessed as I'd never seen him before.

"Is it that obvious?" he chuckled. "Though you must be used to seeing who comes and goes around here. I hope I'm not getting you in trouble by monopolizing your time." And then it hit me. He thought that I was a servant! Perhaps, this assumption was a good thing, I quickly surmised. It would be undignified for a commoner to spend time with a Princess, so maybe it was better that I not reveal to him the truth just yet.

"No, it's fine," I assured him. "I answer to no one, but the Queen." Was I lying by omission? I decided I didn't care.

"Good for you," he said, obviously impressed by my level of importance within the kingdom.

After strolling through the garden, we made our way though the hedge labyrinth and into the apple orchard. We kept walking further and further away from the palace, and my spirit began to feel more free with every step. During most of our walk, we didn't speak, but it didn't feel awkward. I felt like he was having entire conversations with me through his eyes and smile. The apple blossoms had recently bloomed and as the breeze blew, the petals fell to the ground like snowflakes. The air was fragrant and the trees were so lovely that the sight of them made my heart feel lighter. As I looked at my companion, a thought suddenly occurred to me. "Oh my goodness! I've not asked you for your name!"

His face suddenly grew pale as he said, "Why don't you just call me the name that you think suits me best, and I will do the same for you. It will be fun." I was certain that he was trying to conceal something, but then he took my hands in his, and I became distracted once more. "I shall call you my little Snowdrop," he announced without pause.

I giggled at how close it was to my real name. "What made you decide so quickly?"

"Standing here among the falling blossoms and staring at your fair face, all I can think about is snow," he confessed.   "Now, Snowdrop, you must do the same for me… when you look at me, what is the first thing that you think?"

Before I could grow too self conscious to refuse an answer, I looked once more into his eyes and was captured by his gaze.   "I think you're…Charming, " was my unabashed reply.

Now it was his turn to laugh.   "I think we've discovered each other's secret name," he joked.

I sighed, as I truly was charmed by this young man.   "Can I tell you another secret?" I asked.

"Anything, Snowdrop," he assured me.

"I've never had a real friend before," I confessed as I thought of the dolls lining my bed.   All of my friends had been make believe, and I wasn't certain I had what it took to be close to anyone.   "I know how pathetic that sounds, but right now, I'm so happy that I don't want this moment to ever end!"   And then as if fate was punishing me for the hundredth time, we heard the roar of thunder in the distance.

"I find nothing about you pathetic, and you needn't worry as you and I will always remain friends.   But come now, we need to return to the palace quickly, before we get soaked."   He grabbed my hand and interlocked his fingers with mine, and we ran and ran as quickly as we could.   I wasn't used to being touched and even though we were being drenched by the now pouring rain, I'd never felt so much joy.

We fled the orchard and bounded back through the garden and into the castle courtyard again. My feet were soggy from racing through puddles, and my clothes were covered in mud. I couldn't figure out how, but Charming's outfit still looked pristine, albeit wet. His hair remained amazing despite the water pelting us. Finally, we made it safely back inside, and after catching my breath, I couldn't help but laugh. "I'm such a mess!" I said genuinely embarrassed.

"Fear not. It takes rain as well as sunshine for a flower to bloom. If it doesn't harm them, it won't hurt you either," declared Charming. His kind words made me smile once again.

Before we could resume our conversation, a servant emerged and shouted at me, "There you are! We've been looking for you everywhere. The Queen says that dinner is in one hour; you need to change your clothes at once!"

"I'm sorry," I called to Charming as I was being dragged away. "I need to go."

"But when will I see you again?" he asked desperately.

"Oh, dear...I don't know." I was being hurried along and couldn't think clearly.

"Meet me at midnight, back at the well...even if it's still raining. Promise me!"

"Okay, I promise." And then I was at the top of the main staircase and shuffled towards my bedroom by the exasperated servant.

Once I was alone in my room, I wondered if the day had all been a dream. Then I caught a glimpse of myself in my dressing mirror and couldn't help but smile. I was soaked from head to toe, but there was a glow about me I hadn't noticed earlier. Maybe this stranger had placed a charm on me after all. Even though I should have looked like a complete disaster, I felt I had never looked as beautiful as I did at that moment.

I undressed and began to warm myself at the fireplace. Outside I could hear the wind gusting and the rain still pouring. I suddenly felt quite cozy combing out my hair and wondering what to wear. I didn't really care what I looked like for dinner, but I would be meeting Charming at midnight. Since he already saw me looking my worse, I was certain anything would be an improvement. Even so, I wanted to look my very best. I shuffled through the gowns in my wardrobe and finally settled on a red one because it matched my lip color so well. I put on a garnet necklace and some satin heels, and one would never guess that I had been covered in mud just an hour ago.

As I made my way to the banquet hall, I wondered what the occasion was. The Queen rarely dined in my company. I braced myself for another battle. No matter what, I would not allow her to ruin my otherwise perfect day.

The Queen was already sitting at the head of the table when I entered the room. "Snow White, won't you come sit by my side?"

"Yes, Stepmother," said I as I took my seat on the velvet cushioned chair.

"You look quite acceptable tonight," she announced in a way that I couldn't determine was meant to be a compliment or an insult.

"Thank you," I replied.

"We have guests joining us this evening from a nearby kingdom. Relations between us have been strained since your father insulted their King by sending a hunting party onto their land."

"Oh, I'm certain, father didn't know he was trespassing," I declared in his defense.

"A King should be well aware of the borders of his kingdom! Even worse is the fact that he made no act of retribution for the animals that were slaughtered when the incident was brought to his attention. He's been dead five years, and it falls on me to continue to clean up the messes he created," she said with obvious disgust.

"Do you really think tonight's banquet will make amends?" I asked hopeful.

"Well, of course not! They're looking for a bold move on our part to mend our previous alliance. That's why their King sent his only son to negotiate the matter personally."

"What do you plan to offer him?" I asked out of curiosity.

"The hand of our Princess in marriage," the Queen spoke matter-of-factly.

My heart instantly dropped. "Me?" I said incredulous. "You're selling out me over a misunderstanding such as this?" I was completely horrified. That very morning, I might have jumped at the chance to leave the Queen behind and start a new life somewhere else.   Now, all I could think about was seeing Charming again; surely no man could be as handsome and kind as he was!   I no longer wanted a marriage of convenience - to escape one nightmare for one slightly more appealing. Charming was making me remember my childhood dreams of love and happiness.   How could I have forgotten them for even a moment?   My chin began to quiver as I fought back tears.   My stepmother looked at me from the corner of her eye and smiled cruelly.

Just then the courtier appeared to announce the arrival of our royal guests.   I stood up with everyone else, but my eyes remained staring at my place setting.   I did not want to make eye contact with this pompous prince.

"Welcome, my friends," the Queen said in a voice full of joy.   "Let me introduce you to my stepdaughter, Princess Snow..."

"Drop!" I heard a familiar voice exclaim.   My head instantly jerked up, and I locked eyes with my friend from earlier who seemed as stunned as I was.

The Queen, seeing the recognition on my face, calmly inquired, "Have you already met Prince..."

"Charming!" I blurted out.   There he was standing directly across from me.

"Yes, we met earlier today, but I did not know she was the Princess," Charming explained to the Queen.

"Nor I, that he was a Prince," I added.

"Yes, well, let's be seated and enjoy this feast," the Queen suggested.

As enthralled as I was to have Charming here, I needed to remain guarded with the Queen. If she knew how ecstatic I was at the prospect of being his bride, she would do anything in her power to prevent it. The truth was already slipping out, and I needed to do damage control.

"You seem to be glad to see each other once more," the Queen observed.

"No, not really," I spoke before Charming could. "I was just surprised that he's here."

"So then you didn't get along earlier?" asked the Queen.

"I thought we did," Charming interjected, clearly hurt by my nonchalance.

"Then you were mistaken," I said as I waged a war within myself. I lied to the Queen while hoping that Charming would look into my eyes and understand the truth.

"I guess I was," he said, clearly unable to receive my telepathic message.

The rest of dinner was a series of terse words between us. The Queen was once again smiling with satisfaction.

As dinner concluded, the prince stood up and said, "Thank you, your Majesty, for the delicious meal. If you'll excuse me, I'd like to retire to my room; it's been a long day."

"Of course," the Queen replied. "We were honored to have you join us this evening." The Prince didn't even give me a final glance as he retreated from the room.

"May I be excused as well, stepmother?"   I asked, hoping I could intercept Charming in the hallway.

"Don't be foolish, child!   We haven't had dessert yet," she declared, clearly suspicious of my motives.

"I'm not certain I've saved room, but I will happily keep you company while you enjoy yours," I offered, so she might not suspect how eager I was to leave.

"Thank you, Snow.   That will be most agreeable," she decided to my own dismay.   As usual, it was merely words spoken between us.   She didn't really want me by her side anymore than I wanted to be there.   I often wondered if the servants believed the cordial façade we maintained.

The evening seemed to drag on endlessly.   At last, the dishes were cleared, and I bade the Queen "goodnight" and escaped to my room.   It was nearly midnight, and I now had little hope that Charming would still rendezvous with me at the well.   Even so, I grabbed a cloak and slipped outside to wait for him.

It was chilly and still drizzling rain.   I had a lantern, but it was so foggy, I could barely see a foot in front of me.   I waited a long while, thinking of how it would all be in vain.   He would never be interested in me again after the way I treated him this evening!

"Snowdrop, I didn't expect to find you here," I heard a familiar voice whisper through the mist.

"Charming, thank goodness!" I said as I tried to make out his form through the grey haze.   "Please let me explain...I didn't mean anything that I said to you this evening at dinner."

"And what would compel you to lie?"   he questioned as he stood beside me.   I could now see his face by the light of the lantern and his eyes looked both furious and confused.

"The Queen and I have a complicated relationship.   If she knew that I liked you, she would never allow us to see each other again.   But if she thinks that I despise you, she will do anything in her power to make me your bride.   You have to believe me!"

"What exactly are your true feelings?" he demanded.

"I like you very much," I blushed with the confession.   "I would happily run off with you to your kingdom this very night, if you asked me!"

"Snowdrop, I'm not certain what kind of game the Queen and you are playing with one another, but I know better than to be put into the middle. I was sent here to negotiate peace between our lands.   If there is a civil war brewing within this kingdom, I will be unable to take sides.   You need to resolve your issues with the Queen.   Only then can we resume our friendship in an honest manner."

"But you don't understand!" I pleaded.   "I am a prisoner of the Queen's here.   I have no power; everyone follows her commands blindly. We will never be able to resolve our differences!"

"You need more confidence, Snowdrop.   As a Prince, I am working hard to bring peace to my kingdom; as a Princess, you should be working towards that same goal."

Tears now began to trickle down my cheeks.   He would not rescue me from the Queen.   He wanted me to save myself, and I didn't think that I could.

"Snowdrop, I believe in you," he assured me as he held me in his strong arms.   "You can do this."

"For you, I will try."

"Don't do it for me - do it for yourself!   It's unbecoming for a Princess to play petty mind games with her stepmother."

"You must understand that there are years of animosity between us. Even if I make an effort to mend our differences, I'm not convinced that she will."

"You'll never know unless you try.   Be brave and stand proudly; you are the sweet and fair Princess of this land.   I will return before long to witness your progress."

"I promise to try my best," I said as I attempted to muster a smile.

"You'll do great!" he said confidently.   "My men and I will be gone before sunrise, so let me bid you farewell for now."   He embraced me once more and was about to kiss my forehead when I pushed him away.

"I'll see you when you return, provided I'm still alive," I announced melodramatically, before I turned to leave.   I hoped my words would make Charming feel bad, but at the time, I had no idea how close to the truth they would be.

Do What You Have to Do

"The yearning to be near you, I do what I have to do,

but I have the sense to recognize that I don't know how to let you go."

-Sarah McLachlan

The following morning, I found that Charming made good on his word and had left before sunrise.   When they dropped off my breakfast tray, I heard the servants whispering to one another about the sudden departure of the handsome Prince.   I stared at the tray, and there sat a bowl of plain porridge as usual.

"Excuse me," I said as the servants were exiting.   They stopped and turned to see if I was addressing them, though there was no one else present that I could be.   "Please take this porridge back to the kitchen and bring me a strawberry tart with cream instead."   They both stared at me blankly.   "We had them for dessert last night," I explained, "and I was too full to eat mine.   I'd like to have it this morning for breakfast."

"The Queen said that you are to have porridge," one of them said as if her word was sacred.

This made me snap.   "I am the Princess, and I do not want porridge: not this morning, not tomorrow morning, and never again!   Go bring me back a strawberry tart at once!"

"Yes, your highness," they said with a curtsey and then hurried away with the breakfast tray.

As I awaited their return, I opened the curtains and was surprised to see that the sun was shining brightly.   After all the rain from the previous day, I could make out a faint rainbow on the horizon.   I took it as a sign of a new beginning.   My life was made of sunshine and rain, just like Charming said.   Whatever storm ahead I faced with the Queen, I was certain I could weather it.   I'd remained complacent too long; today would be a day of changes.

The servants returned with my breakfast tray and set it on my sitting table.   "Thank you," I said happily as I sat down to eat.   Then I spotted it. "Wait!"   I said, halting the women once more.   "This is an apple tart; I did not ask for apple."

"It was all they had left," one of the servants said.

"Really?" I asked in disbelief.   I knew that there had been a plate stacked high with them that were left untouched at the banquet.

"Well, the Queen asked that all the strawberry ones be saved for her alone," the other servant admitted.

"We'll see about that!"   I said as the two women looked at each other with large, worried eyes.   "You are dismissed!"

"Yes, your highness," they said in unison as they eagerly retreated.

I opened my wardrobe and pulled out a deep purple, embroidered gown.   It definitely invoked royalty and thus would be my uniform to confront the Queen.   I put on high heels that made me stand straighter and appear taller.   I placed a crystal tiara in my raven hair.   I sneered once more at the apple tart as I marched quickly and with purpose towards the Queen's chambers.

I knocked on the door to her wing of the castle and a servant opened it timidly.

"Oh, Princess!"   she said in surprise.   "I'll let the Queen know you are requesting an audience with her."

"Let me through," I said as I shoved my way past her.

"Wait!   Protocol dictates..." she began.

I turned to face her.   "I'm the Princess.   I make rules - not follow them."

I kept on walking as a line of servants now followed, hoping to intervene, but also fearful of opposing me.   I threw open the door to her bedroom, but she was not inside.   Then I ran to the library with the same result.   Finally, I marched into her sitting room, and there she sat, drinking a cup of tea.

Her lady in waiting immediately ran in front of me and said, "Your highness, we were not expecting you!   If you'd like to speak to the Queen, we can make arrangements.   She is eating her breakfast right now and does not wish to be disturbed."

"She is eating <u>my</u> breakfast, you mean," I shouted as I lunged for a strawberry tart.

The Queen let out an amused cackle.   "It's alright, ladies.   If you'll excuse us, I'd like my stepdaughter to join me for breakfast."   The servants all bowed and left.   Then to me, she said, "Sit down, my dear."

"No thank you, I'd prefer to stand," I said defiantly before I began to devour the scrumptious pastry.   The Queen poured me a cup of tea. Since she wasn't expecting me, I decided it couldn't be poisoned and took a sip.

"So, what brings you here?" the Queen humored me.

"I'm never eating porridge again," I informed her.   "It is not for you to decide what I will eat.   If I want to eat strawberry tarts to my heart's content, I shall do so."

"Very well," the Queen smirked.   "Now cut the pretense...you're not really here about pastries, are you?" she asked with a knowing glance.

For the first time since I stood facing her, my stomach dropped and fear began to seep within me.   To argue about trivialities was one thing, but to cut to the heart of the matter was quite another.   I wasn't sure how best to proceed.

I stood there frozen long enough that she decided to venture her own guess.   "Snow White, is this morning's intrusion directly correlated to the conversation   we were having last night about the possibility of you marrying the Prince?"

"That is part of it," I decided.

"Well, speak up, child!   What is it you need to say?" she demanded.

"I want a voice in who I marry," I declared.   "I don't want to be used as a pawn to avoid conflict or awarded to a man as some sort of prize."

"But you are the Princess," she reminded me. "You must make choices based on the good of your kingdom regardless of your own feelings."

"Not always," I maintained. "I have already suffered enough, and I refuse to be unhappy forever. Someday I will marry the man that I love; it's what my father would have wanted."

"Your father did not want to die, but he did. We do not always get what we want, whether it is fair or not, you realize," the Queen said solemnly. I sensed that she was not really speaking about my father at all, but something in her own mysterious personal history.

"I understand that there are circumstances beyond our control. I'm simply asking for more control over my own destiny in situations that allow it," I managed to explain.

I felt good about opening up and for once being honest with the Queen, until I saw the look on her face begin to contort. Something I had said clearly struck a nerve.

"Are you challenging me, Snow White?" the Queen wanted to know. "As Princess, are you trying to take control of the kingdom of Whitebirchburg away from its Queen?"

"No, you misunderstand," I said now frightened to go toe to toe against the Queen. "What I want is for us to work together for the good of both of us, as well as the kingdom. I'm no longer a child and can now be trusted with more responsibility. I feel that you and I have never really been honest with each other, and I'm ready to put the past behind us and start anew."

At first, the Queen seemed taken aback by my suggestion. Then she sat in silence a full minute, sipping her tea and seemingly lost in thought. At last, she looked up at me and smiled gently. "You may be right, my dear stepdaughter. You are a young woman now, and I need to acknowledge it. As a sign of trust, I will allow you to help me in the matter at hand. The Prince departed with his entourage early this morning. Although he acted gracious by our hospitality, the past actions of the King clearly remain unforgiven ."

"Would you like me to travel to his kingdom and apologize to their King in person?" I asked eagerly.

"Don't be foolish, Snow White. If you went marching down there, who's to say they won't hold you captive for a ransom? We must act carefully. Obviously, the incident warrants further investigation. I will arrange for you to meet with the royal huntsman who was in charge the day this all took place. Perhaps, he can clarify if and why the King was hunting in someone else's territory, and you can determine what can be offered in retribution."

"I would be honored to help you in this affair, stepmother," I said and meant it. She went from offering my hand in marriage as a quick fix to allowing me to head an investigation and find an alternative solution. Perhaps, Charming had been right about us settling our differences.

"I'll send for you later," she said and smiled once more.

"I look forward to it," I said with a curtsy and then returned to my own room. I had sudden respect for the Queen, which was most unexpected. I guess she wasn't as unreasonable as I had thought.

When I looked out my window, the sun was now hidden by dark clouds.   I let out a sigh, hoping that it wouldn't rain again.   Then I spotted the apple tart still set upon the table.   I'd now had my fill of strawberry and decided that it did in fact look good, so I sat down to eat it as well.   Yet when I bit into it, something tasted wrong.   The spicy cinnamon apple flavor left me feeling unsatisfied rather than content, as the strawberries and cream had.   And all at once it crept in - doubt.   Was the Queen testing me?   Was she setting me up for failure so that the people of this land would turn against me?   I was no longer sure what to think.   So, I abandoned the pastry and decided to find something else to occupy my time.

I worked on my needlepoint in order to calm my nerves.   Normally, I found it to be a soothing, mindless activity, but in my current state of agitation, I kept pricking my finger on the needle.   As I saw a drop of blood pucker to the surface of my finger, I decided to abandon the project and go for a walk in the garden instead.   I put on my wool cloak since there was still a chill in the air.   As I paced the rose garden, the memory of Charming was still so vivid and fresh in my mind.   Before long, I had forgotten all about my breakfast with the Queen and was instead daydreaming about my next encounter with the Prince.

Reality came crashing in as the Queen's lady in waiting approached me in the garden.   "Your highness, the Queen is summoning you to her throne room," she spoke in an official tone.

This would be the moment that would change everything, I decided.

If all went well, my relationship with the Queen would be mended, Charming would approve of me as a capable woman, and I would gain confidence to act as Princess of Whitebirchburg.   There was so much to be gained, and yet the anticipation was rapidly transforming into nervousness. Still, my feet carried me to the throne room where the Queen sat perched above me.   The royal huntsman was already present.

"Ah, Snow White, there you are," the Queen said approvingly.   "This is the huntsman who accompanied your father on the day in question.   He is requesting that he bring you to the exact location so you can discern if there was trespassing taking place or not."

"Very well," I said to the Queen and then to the huntsman, "I greatly appreciate your assistance."

"I am honored to accompany the Princess," he said in a deep, coarse voice.   "I have the necessary maps of the kingdom in my saddlebag.   Shall we depart at once?"

"Absolutely," I said as we headed to the stables.   I didn't dare to look at the Queen as we left.   I somehow feared she wore the familiar smirk that would only intimidate me.

There was a black horse speckled with white that had been saddled for me.   "His name is Starburst," the stable boy informed me.   As I mounted the steed, I noticed that he seemed a bit skittish.

"It's okay, Starburst," I assured him.   I'd always felt a kinship to animals, because they have a way of behaving in a manner more patient and kind than most people I knew.   So, I felt certain that I could keep my horse calm during our journey.

"Princess, follow my lead," the huntsman called to me from his horse. We traveled northeast all day, and I secretly began to worry that we would not reach the spot we needed to by sunset. Eventually, the huntsman came to a halt and dismounted his horse. I slowed Starburst down from his steady, rapid pace.

"Are we there?" I asked a bit anxious.

"Not yet, your highness, but there is a brook here that has fresh water, and I thought you might be getting thirsty," he explained.

I climbed off Starburst's back, but remained by his side to alleviate his nervousness. The huntsman had dipped a pewter cup into the stream and handed it to me to drink.

"Thank you," I said and then took a cool, refreshing swallow. I guess I hadn't realized how dehydrated I had become, but I quickly drank the entire cup. "We really shouldn't rest for long, but I am glad that we stopped," I confessed. "I didn't notice how tired I was before, but now I'm truly exhausted."

"Why don't you sit down on the bank?" the huntsman suggested as he filled his canteen.

"Yes, I think I will," I said as I removed my cloak and sat on top of it. My eyelids were growing heavier by the second, so I closed them, thinking I would rest for just a minute. I probably should've been alarmed by the sudden exhaustion, but instead, I felt quite peaceful. I must have fallen asleep, though I don't remember it. I do know that I heard Starburst whinny, and I awoke in time to see him bucking, run in a full circle and finally, flee.

"No, Starburst! Come back!" I shouted.

"Don't worry about him; he's not needed anymore," the huntsman said to me.

"Not needed? What do you mean?" I asked and then realized the horrible truth. There was rope and a dagger resting on the ground by my side. The huntsman had just scared my horse away. Clearly he had slipped something in my drink that was disorienting and sleep inducing when he handed me that cup. He unquestionably meant to do me harm!

Though I felt dizzy, I had a surge of adrenaline rushing through my veins. I grabbed the dagger and started running as if my life depended upon it, because, in fact, it did. I knew that my best chance of survival would be to hide, as I could not outrun a strong man in my current state. I left the dirt road we were on and headed towards the dense forest. A heel had already broken off one of my shoes, causing me to trip over tree roots and pine cones. I tossed the shoe and continued on, not daring to stop, even though I knew I was sure to become lost. I couldn't even process why this was happening. It simply didn't make sense for this man to have lured me so far from home. What possible reason could he have to kill me?

After running for what felt like an eternity, I spotted a large tree toppled over and resting on a boulder. There was enough room between the log and the ground for someone in small stature to hide beneath. I piled leaves and debris on top of myself to conceal my purple dress and laid as still as I possibly could, afraid that even my breathing would give me away.

I could still feel the effects of the drug I'd been given. I was sleepy once more, but was too afraid to close my eyes in case I had ingested poison and would never awake again. I tried to focus my eyes on the log above me and when a wood spider came crawling by, I stifled a scream. So, I dug my fingers into the cool dirt underneath me and felt for pebbles. I would count how many I could find and concentrate on that and nothing else. Anytime I heard a movement, I would freeze. Sometimes, a squirrel would wander by or occasionally a bird would perch on the log before flying away. I kept fearing that I would be found, but time began to pass, and it grew darker by the minute. Night was descending, and it occurred to me how hungry I had become. I would now do just about anything for the apple tart I had scorned this morning. I'd never been so hungry and tired in all my life. It soon became impossible for me to remain conscious and sleep overtook me at last.

Fighter

"Cause it makes me that much stronger, makes me work a little bit harder,

It makes me that much wiser, so thanks for making me a fighter."

- Christina Aguilera

When I opened my eyes, I was back in the apple orchard with Charming, but the trees were now heavy with fruit, ripe enough to be picked.

"Snowdrop, why have you summoned me here?" he asked with deep concern.

"You told me you would not pick sides, but you must! I'm asking you to pick mine," I demanded of him.

"Are you in trouble?" he asked as if he already feared the answer he would hear.

"Yes," I replied. "I need you to come rescue me. It's imperative that you hurry!"

"How? What am I supposed to do?" asked he desperately.

I reached for a round, red apple and plucked it from its swaying branch. "Eat this," I insisted as I handed the piece of fruit to him. "It will give you the knowledge of all you need to find me again."

He bit into the apple and swallowed.   Then he looked directly into my eyes and said, "I understand."

At that moment, I awoke, still buried in the crevice.   I remembered at once what had transpired the day before.   I realized that the potion in my drink must have been designed to make me sleep, not to kill me as I had originally feared.   I thought about my dream and wished that Charming would receive my message to him, though I knew that it was quite impossible.

My stomach growled at me like a vicious animal, and I knew that I had to find something edible to abate the hunger.   I would have to tread carefully, in case, the huntsman was still on the prowl.   I pondered whether I should remain hidden awhile longer or venture out to locate food. In the end, my stomach won out over my brain.

I carefully crawled out of the ditch and shook off the leaves that were sticking to my dress.   There were no animals in sight - no squirrels, no chipmunks, not even any birds perching in the trees.   The quiet was unsettling.   Then I knew why the animals had fled.

"Did you think I wouldn't find you?   I'm a tracker by profession," the huntsman's voice boomed from behind me.   I turned around and saw him standing there with my broken shoe in his hands.

"If you kill me, the Queen will have your head!" I threatened.

The huntsman glared at me, then shook his head in disbelief.   "Stupid wench, you haven't figured it out yet, have you?   I'm following her orders -

the Queen is the one who wants you dead!"

"Liar!" I shouted, but I knew inside that he spoke the truth. It was what I had feared all along. I should have made Charming understand the real situation when I had the chance.

"She's the one who gave me the potion to knock you out. I planned to have my way with you before slitting your throat. The Queen only requested that I bring back your heart for proof of your demise."

I instinctively started backing up slowly. I knew I couldn't run or hide, so I now felt that my best option was to reason with this disgusting man. I made my attempt.

"You don't have to go through with it now. I'm not going to return to the castle ever again. I've always known that the Queen hated me, so I promise to keep away forever."

"Poor little rich girl, you're better off dead than left to wander these woods alone! You'd starve to death or be attacked by wild animals. I'm the good guy - putting you out of your misery and sending you straight to heaven!"

I then realized I'd made a critical error; you can't rationalize with a crazy man! So, I turned to flee, but he caught me by my right arm and twisted it behind my back as he threw me hard against a nearby tree trunk. He grabbed his rope and began to tie me to the tree, but my left hand was still free to grab the dagger I had tucked inside the sash of my gown.

"I can't wait to skin you like a rabbit," he whispered in my ear as he knotted the first length of rope. He was close enough to me that I thrust the dagger as hard as I could into his abdomen.   I yanked it back out as he howled backwards in pain and cut the rope with the bloodied blade.   I knew this would slow him down, but probably wouldn't end his pursuit.   I looked around and scanned my surroundings.   I picked up a large granite rock and aimed for his head.   I heard his skull crack and more yelping in agony as I ran away.

I wanted to run all the way to Charming's kingdom, except that I was now so lost, I had no idea where my current location was, let alone which direction to go.   I stopped to remove my one good shoe, but carried it with me as I refused to leave any clues to my whereabouts this time.   A loop of rope still hung on my right wrist, chafing the skin.   The crystal tiara hung off my scraggly hair.   A bruise swelled on my right cheek and my jaw was sore from being thrown against the tree.   It was then that I decided for sure that I would not be going to heaven just yet.   I could not meet my mother looking like this!

So, the will to survive kept my heart beating even as my feet ached with every step I took.   I couldn't be sure if the huntsman was still alive, so I would assume the worse and believe that he was still tailing me.

As the day dragged on, I began to feel sick and dizzy.   I wasn't sure if it was because I was so badly dehydrated and starving, the effects of the potion had not fully worn off, or the stress of the situation that was keeping me on edge.   I was so weary that even the tree branches began to resemble human hands reaching out to grab me.   I was about to pass out when I found a patch of wild blackberries that I ate ravenously.   When I had finished, I worried that I had paused too long.   I reminded myself that I was being hunted and needed to keep moving.   So I grabbed my shoe with my purple stained fingers and began to run once more.

The light of the sun danced between the tree branches and shone on a rickety cottage in the midst of this fearsome forest.   At first, I thought it might be a trick of light, but as I approached the door, I discovered that it was very much real.   I knocked as loud as my worn out body would allow, but there was no response.   I turned the door knob, and it was unlocked, so I made my way inside.

"Hello!   Is anybody here?" I asked as a reluctant, but desperate trespasser.   I received no answer.   This house was a sanctum of respite and perhaps if I waited for the owner to return and shared my tale, I would be offered a bed or a meal or some other assistance.   That was my plan, so I decided to sit on a kitchen stool and wait.

As I sat there catching my breath, my eyes began to wander and for the first time I really saw where I was.   There were dead birds hanging from the ceiling and jars containing animal parts and liquids lining a dusty, old shelf.   On the walls were drawn grids and diagrams in chalk, and the cauldron on the fire permeated a foul odor.   There were candles arranged on the tips of a star that was painted on the kitchen table, as well as a stain of blood.   I had no knowledge of black magick, but even I could sense the evil aura looming in this room.

Panic seized me once more, and I knew I needed to leave before someone came home to torture and sacrifice me to some dark God.   Was it wrong that even surrounded by such vile sights and scared to be discovered, my stomach still begged for sustenance?

I decided that I needed to take my chances and eat something before leaving.   So I went to the pantry shelf and found a sack of cracked walnuts. If I only took a few, no one would ever notice, right?   Then I saw a shelf with day old bread and a plate of cheese.   I tore off large chunks of both and devoured them quickly.   As I began to eat, I realized that it would be obvious that someone had consumed the food, so I decided there was no sense in hiding the fact.   My insatiable appetite was not abated until I ate the entire loaf of bread and most of the cheese.   There was a pitcher of what appeared to be water on the counter, but having already been drugged once, I decided not to take my chances.   I found a bottle of wine and drank that instead.

Now with a full belly, my first instinct should have been to run, but I then decided that if the owner was going to cast a hex on me for stealing, I ought to make it count as much as possible.   So I dared to climb the staircase to the bedroom and looked for something more suitable to wear. I took off the heavy, purple garment I was wearing and tried on a lovely dress with a gold colored skirt and a contrasting blue bodice.   I removed the crystal tiara and fixed a red ribbon in my hair to keep it out of my face. Finally, I grabbed a pair of simple shoes that felt like pillows on my blistered, bare feet.

Then I got on the floor and knelt in prayer.   "Dear Lord, I know that stealing is an unforgivable sin, but right now I am trying to just survive.

Please let this disguise help me deceive the huntsman if I encounter him again.   Bless the strange woman who lives here that I have trespassed against; I am certain that she is in need of my prayers.   Give me the opportunity to repent for my transgressions and allow me to be more the person that you mean for me to be each day.   Amen."

I got up and hurried down the stairs as I carried my gown, broken shoe and tiara.   I found a cape that I wrapped them all in and decided to carry some food with me as well.   I returned to the pantry and grabbed two cucumbers and a sweet potato.   When I spotted some dried apple slices, my stomach churned and I knew that I had overextended my welcome and should flee with what I had or risk putting myself in additional danger.

I sprinted from the broken down cottage as quickly as I could, growing ever nervous that I might run into its owner on my way.   At first, I followed a nearby stream, but then decided I might be too likely to encounter someone on this path.   I took the opportunity to wash the blood stained dagger in the brook before heading into the woods once more.

Carrying the clothes and food was a heavy load in my frail condition, plus the wine was now making me drowsy.   But I didn't dare to rest and continued on through sunset, twilight and then by moonlight.

Eventually, I reached a mountainside and by the light of a nearly full moon, I could spot the entrance of a cave.   I decided that this was as fine a place as any to take shelter for the night.   When I went inside, I tripped over something.   I picked it up and by the glint of moon beams saw that it was a pickax.   This gave me an idea.   I counted fifty paces from the cave entrance and dug a hole in the ground deep enough to bury my dress, shoe and tiara.   After covering them with dirt, I put on the cape and carried the vegetables back to the cave.   I cut cucumber slices with the dagger, and they tasted so refreshing after such a long day.   Then I lied down on the cold stone ground with the pickax and dagger by my side for protection. Despite the lack of comfort, I was so sore and tired that I fell asleep more easily than expected.

I don't remember what I dreamed that night, but while I was in a drowsy stupor of being half awake and half asleep, I heard the sound of voices hovering over me.

"Somebody's here."   "It's a girl!"   "What is she doing here?"   "Is she a thief?"   "Is she injured?"

I cradled the dagger in my hand and opened my eyes to find seven dwarfs staring down at me.   Even though they were little, they clearly had me outnumbered, so I held out the dagger at arms length menacingly. "Keep away from me!" I warned as I stood up.

"Whoa, Miss," one of them addressed me.   "Just calm down.   We mean you no harm."

"What are you doing here?" I asked.

Another one answered in a huffy tone, "Us?   This is our land!   The real question is what are you doing here?"

"I just needed a place to sleep last night and will now be on my way," I assured him.

"Oh, my!   Are you a fugitive on the run?" the first one asked me.

41

"You didn't come to steal from us - did you?" another one inquired.

"Gosh, you're too pretty to be a criminal," one of the others said.

Their intrigue in my situation was starting to amuse me.   I realized that they weren't going to hurt me, so I put the dagger back in the sash of my dress.   "What could I possibly steal from a cave?" I asked, giggling at their assessment of thievery which had in fact become my most recent occupation.

"This isn't merely a cave; it's a mine!" one of them proudly announced.

"Hmph!   We shouldn't trust her.   The only reason a woman would come here is to steal our gems!" the surly one scolded.

"Wow!   A jewel thief sounds like an exciting life!   Would you tell us all about it?" one of them insisted.

"Well," I began, "my story does have adventure, but not in the way you think."   The dwarfs stared at me mesmerized.   Although I was reluctant to trust strangers, I sensed that these men were kind and might help me. So I decided that sharing the truth would be more sensible than telling a lie. We all stepped outside and sat down in a circle on the ground.

"My name is Snow White, and I was Princess of this kingdom until my stepmother, the Queen, tried to have me killed by the royal huntsman. I've been wandering lost in the woods ever since I made my escape.   I fear that my life is still in danger, and that the Queen will not be satisfied until I am dead.   I have no allies to rely upon in my time of need.   Will you all please help me?"

The dwarfs sat there with jaws dropped.   "You're the Princess?"

"The Queen mustn't get away with this!"   "We can hide you away at our house!"

"Oh, I would be so grateful if you would let me stay with you for awhile," I said with sincere enthusiasm.

"If she stays at our cottage, she must remain concealed inside so no spies of the Queen will find her," one of them said to the others in a serious tone.

"Well, let's head there at once!" another declared.   "There's no time to waste!"   "Hurry, Princess!"   "Let's be on our way!"

So, I followed their lead as my weary body kept pace with their short legs.   Before long, we were at a quaint cottage by a rushing stream.   After fleeing the rickety home yesterday, this house looked like a vision of tranquility.   I had no idea that this peaceful abode would soon feel more like a prison to me.

Sweet Dreams

"Everybody's looking for something, Some of them want to use you,

Some of them want to be used by you."   - Annie Lennox

Being accustomed to palace living, the cottage of the seven dwarfs seemed to me a dirty hovel as I entered their home.   Still, it beat sleeping in a ditch or a cave, so I bit my tongue and didn't complain.   The dwarfs were generous to let me stay with them when it meant their own lives were now in danger.   It was probably this fear of what the Queen might do to those helping the fugitive Princess that motivated them to keep me concealed in their home at all costs.

The morning I arrived, they bolted the windows.   They didn't have curtains, but nailed pieces of fabric in place so no sunlight could peek inside. They gave me some bread and a mug with water.

"Do you have a kettle?   I'll make us some tea," I offered.   They looked at each other and shrugged.   Two of them began looking through an assortment of pots and pans to no avail.   Tea was now a luxury I would have to do without.

I sat on a tiny chair and looked around at my surroundings.   All the furniture looked custom built for the dwarfs' small size.   Their home might actually be quite adorable if it wasn't so messy and neglected.   When they

left for work, I would surprise them by cleaning it up, I decided.   The bread
was hard, and I had to dunk it in the water just to make it edible.   It was
overwhelming to think that my life had come to this - running for my life,
relying on the hospitality of strangers, cleaning when I always had others
tidy up for me, and eating whatever was available whether it tasted good or
not.   Was I really the same girl who was demanding strawberry tarts just
days ago?

I was so lost in thought that I hadn't noticed the dwarfs sit down beside
me and begin to silently stare.   I now felt uncomfortable as they watched
intently as I ate.   So, I decided I should make some light conversation.

"You now know who I am, but I know nothing about all of you," I
began.   "Why don't you tell me your names?"

"I'm afraid we can't do that, Princess," one of them replied.

"We call each other by nicknames only.   You can call us whatever you
like," another one said.

"But why?" I asked, puzzled.

"If no one knows our true name, then it can never be dishonored or
made fun of, so we keep our names secret," still another explained.

"But then your name might never be celebrated either," I reasoned.

"It's the way we were raised, so it's not strange to us.   We rather
enjoy being called by several names," one of them admitted.

"Well, whatever makes you happy," I smiled.

"So, tell us, Princess, how can we assist you while you're hiding from
the Queen?" one of them asked.   I was thankful to now discuss practical

matters.

"I need to find my Prince.   Once he understands that I tried to reason with the Queen and my life is now in danger, he'll come to my rescue and never leave my side again," I explained.

"Great!" the dwarf declared.   "What is the Prince's name?"

I paused finally realizing that I didn't know his real name.   "I guess I never learned his actual name..."

"Why not?" someone inquired.

"He also asked that I call him by a nickname," I confessed.   "I only know him as Charming."

"That's okay," one of the dwarfs assured me.   "Just tell us what kingdom he hails from and we can still find him."

"Oh, my goodness!   I have no idea!" I concluded in horror.   "We only met the other day...and I guess I actually know nothing of value about him!" I began to sob in frustration.   All romantic notions of my Prince saving me like a true hero were destroyed as the reality of my situation occurred to me.   "I don't even know what direction to travel to his kingdom.   I truly know nothing!"

"Don't cry, Princess!"   "You've been through a lot, and you need to rest!"   "You'll remember more tomorrow!"   "Just relax!"   "If you keep crying, you'll make us cry too!"   "Please don't be sad, Princess!"

The dwarfs' pleas to stop sobbing guilted me into calming down.   I tried to calculate what my next move was, but came up empty.   There was no one in my palace that I trusted; they all answered to the Queen.   I had

no family to rely on.   I really had no choice but to hide at the dwarfs'
cottage indefinitely.   How long before they, too, grew tired of me?

"Thank you for being so kind to me.   This is a situation I never guessed
I would find myself in," I quietly lamented.

"Will you be okay, Princess, if we leave you here alone and continue
our work for the day?" one dwarf asked.

"Yes, of course," I said actually grateful to have some time to myself.

The moment they exited the cottage, I grabbed a broom and got to
work sweeping the untidy home.   I dusted, removed cobwebs, mopped,
scrubbed, organized the clutter, cleaned and stacked dishes, made beds and
began to make dinner.   All of these tasks were foreign to me, though I'd
watched others do them a thousand times.   Completing each job kept my
mind so preoccupied that I wasn't worrying about my current predicament.

When the little men arrived home, I shouted, "Surprise!   I cleaned up
your house; I sure hope you don't mind."

"It looks wonderful!"   "Thank you, Princess!"   "You didn't have to,
but we're sure glad you did!"   "Something smells good!"

"I made us potato leek soup for supper," I revealed.   "I've never
cooked before, so I hope it tastes alright."

"I'm sure it will be delicious!   But before we eat, we have a surprise
for you, as well," one dwarf spoke as the others smiled.

"What is it?" I wondered aloud.   Then they opened the door and
dragged in a straw stuffed mattress long enough for me.   They must have
spent the day making it.   "A bed for me?   I'll never be able to repay your

kindness," I admitted.

"Just look around - you already have!" "Come, let's eat supper!"

So we sat around their table, as I poured bowls of soup for everyone. It tasted pretty good for a first attempt, but the dwarfs behaved as if it was the best thing they'd ever tasted.   I wasn't sure if they were trying to spare my feelings or if they really were unaccustomed to eating decent food.

Afterwards, they grabbed blankets and pillows and made up my bed in the corner of the room.   Cleaning and cooking had left me exhausted and since I hadn't slept well in two days, I knew I was going to fall asleep instantly.   As soon as the dwarfs retired to their beds upstairs, I laid my head on the pillow and fell asleep.

I made my way back to the palace, growing more determined with every step to confront the Queen.   As I walked through town, there was no one in sight.   The silence was eerie.   When I arrived at the palace gate, nobody was there to welcome or stop me from entering.   As I proceeded to the courtyard, I saw everyone gathered together dressed all in black.   It seemed I showed up to my own memorial service.   My portrait was displayed prominently with flowers arranged all around it.   Next to it stood my stepmother telling the people that their Princess had been lost in the woods and was presumed to be deceased.   I walked over to the platform where she stood as the crowd parted for me to make my way.

When I reached my stepmother, I turned to the crowd and said, "Fear not, your Princess is alive and well!"   There was an eruption of cheers.   I turned to the Queen, knowing that she would have to embrace me to save face in the eyes of the public.

She wrapped her arms around me and whispered, "If you didn't have the good sense to die, you should have at least known better than to return here." And then she yanked a sharp blade into my back. I screamed in horror as I heard the crowd cheer again, this time for my destruction. Then I quickly blacked out.

I awoke in a cold sweat, gasping for breath and trying to make sense of whether I was alive or dead. I had hoped such a nightmare would be a one time occurrence due to the initial discomfort of the straw mattress after sleeping my entire life upon goose feather down pillows.

Unfortunately, the theme of the dream was recurring. Each night, I would fall asleep and imagine myself returning to the palace. The details would vary - sometimes the guards would escort me to the Queen's throne room, other times I would find her in the banquet hall or waiting for me in my own bedroom. At times, a crowd would be present, other times we would be all alone. But every time I confronted the Queen, she would kill me. I'd been bludgeoned, beaten, choked, stabbed, beheaded, hanged, smothered and burned. I experienced over a hundred deaths since my arrival at the dwarfs' cottage.

My days were fast becoming a nightmare as well. At first, I didn't mind cooking and cleaning, but soon the dwarfs were expecting me to take on more unsuitable tasks. They made me mend their clothes, launder their bed sheets and garments, kill the mice invading their home, and sing them to sleep at night.   I was forced to be a maid, chef, exterminator and entertainer all in one, when I was, in fact, none of these things.

As I set about these tasks, I would consider who I really was.   I was a Princess without a kingdom, which meant I essentially had no purpose.   I wasn't a daughter, or a sister, or a niece, or a wife, or an aunt, or a mother. I wasn't anyone to anybody.   I was still a woman, of course, but what exactly was the value of that?   So far, it meant that disgusting men like the huntsman would try to rape me if given the opportunity and that even the dwarfs would take advantage of me by transforming me into their servant. Even Charming failed to take me seriously, which is why I was now living in the woods instead of with him.

I continued my chores as my depression festered and my frustration became unbearable.   This cottage had lost its quaint appeal and now felt like a prison.   The dwarfs would not allow me to step outside in case I should be spotted.   Every now and then, I would lift the cloth off the window pane and stare at the birds flying in the sunshine.   I longed for that sense of freedom and wondered what would happen if I left the dwarfs and just started walking once more.   Where would I go?   What adventures might I have?   Then my sensible side would talk me out of it, and the dwarfs would return home hungry for their supper.

I now had names for the dwarfs.   Their physical characteristics and personalities had seeped into the names I created.   There was MisterMaster, who was their unspoken leader, though he seemed unaware of it.   Glumdrops was perpetually gloomy and pessimistic.   Grinny was the polar opposite of Glumdrops and was always happy and looking on the bright side.   Cruncher ate noisily and would have a mound of crumbs at his place setting after eating.   Slackjack was forever tired and never motivated to work hard, like the others.   Patches was constantly tearing holes in his clothing and scraping his knees and elbows.   He was by far the most clumsy in the group.   The lone dwarf without a beard, I called Sillybird because he was so carefree and kind, though definitely not the brightest.   I assumed he was the youngest, though I didn't know for sure.   He never spoke words, but communicated through facial expressions and gestures. I wasn't certain if this was because he didn't know how to speak or was just too shy around me to do so.   I was the most fond of Sillybird, probably because, like me, he fit in the least.

I heard the dwarfs returning home and quickly set the table for dinner.

"We're home, Princess!" MisterMaster proclaimed.

"You're a bit tardy tonight," I scolded.

"Sorry," Cruncher began, "but we stopped to pick this!"   He placed a bucketful of ripe apples onto the counter.

"We figured you could bake us an apple pie tomorrow," Grinny added. I couldn't think of anything I would prefer to do less.

"I have another shirt for you to mend," Patches announced in his nonchalant voice.

"Of course you do," I said as resentment began to creep into my tone.

"Tonight's dinner isn't very good!" Glumdrops announced.

"Then you don't have to eat it!" I shouted as I took his plate and threw it across the room.

"Whoa, Princess!" MisterMaster said.   "Watch your temper; you almost broke that plate!"

"I'm sorry," I said as I got up and went over to examine the plate on the floor.   "I meant to do this!" I exclaimed as I shattered the plate on the floor.

"Nice going," Glumdrops snorted.   "Now you have an even bigger mess to clean up!"

"I'm not your slave!   Clean it up yourself!"   I snapped as I handed him the broom.

Then I reached for the door handle, and for the first time in months, went outside.   I kicked off my shoes and went over to the brook to soak my feet.   I looked at my reflection in the stream and barely recognized myself. My dress was becoming rags, my hands were rough and calloused, and my hair was a mess of tangles.   I let out a scream from the depths of my soul that scared all the wildlife away, except for a raven that stared down at me from its branch as if challenging me to shriek again.

Several of the dwarfs ran outside.   "What are you doing?   You'll blow your cover!" MisterMaster declared.

"Not likely," I replied.   "When I left the palace, it was spring.   The leaves are changing color and the apples are ripe, which means it's now autumn.   I must be assumed dead by now."

"You might be right, but why take the chance?" Slackjack asked.

"Because I'm tired of hiding like a criminal in your house!   I need fresh air!   I need to see the sun and the moon!"

"Fine!   If you need to be outside, please just don't talk to any strangers who wander by.   You never know who might be spying for the Queen," MisterMaster reminded me.

"Why are you so angry, Princess?" Grinny asked.   "Crankypants is always rude," he said, speaking of Glumdrops.

"Well, maybe it's time someone taught him some manners," I insisted. Such a prospect was enough to frighten Sillybird into running back inside the cottage. "You all need to be reminded who I am.   Tomorrow, dig at fifty paces south of the entrance of your mine.   Maybe then you'll remember how I should be treated."   I returned to the cottage.   I patted Sillybird on the head and ignored the dirty dishes.   Glumdrops had finished sweeping up the broken pieces of his dish with a harrumph.   I climbed into bed and prepared to face the Queen again.

I'm Like a Bird

"I only fly away, I don't know where my soul is,

I don't know where my home is."   – Nelly Furtado

The kitchen smelled of sweetness, warmth, and new possibilities.   I baked the dwarfs triberry muffins for breakfast.   I opened the windows, delighting in the sunshine and gentle autumn breeze.   Today would be a new beginning for me.

"Good morning, everyone!" I spoke as I brought the tray of muffins over to the table.

"What's so good about it?" Glumdrops mumbled.

The others ignored his comment and began to eat.   "Princess, these are amazing!"   Cruncher insisted.

"I've never tasted anything so delicious!" Grinny added.

"Oh, I'm so glad you like them," I said in a cheerful manner.   "You can consider it my parting gift to all of you.   I can't thank you enough or ever repay your kindness and hospitality."

"What's this?" MisterMaster asked in confusion.   "You're not thinking of leaving us, are you, Princess?"

"Yes, I think it's time," I said with certainty.

"But it's not safe!" Patches exclaimed.

"Where will you go?" Cruncher wondered.

"Back to the palace," I calmly explained.

"That's crazy!" MisterMaster insisted. "That's the single most dangerous place for you to go! Why would you even think about returning there?"

"Everyone must think I'm dead by now," I reasoned, "including Charming. I need to find him before he gives up on me and falls in love with someone else. I can collect the map I need to find his kingdom at the palace."

"But what if you find him and he has already found someone new?" Glumdrops asked.

"That's a chance I'll have to take," I sighed as my heart pounded in protest at the thought. "He still might be kind enough to hide me within his kingdom's walls and find a job for me to do in order to keep me safe." I found this scenario to be a dreary prospect, but wouldn't admit so to the dwarfs.

"How do you plan to infiltrate the palace?" questioned MisterMaster, who clearly worried that I had not thought my plan out thoroughly.

"I know every inch of the palace grounds. There are a few places I could sneak in without being easily noticed. Once inside, I'll steal a servant's uniform and move about more freely."

"Even still, it's so dangerous!" observed Slackjack.

"If you're discovered, the Queen will surely kill you!" MisterMaster stated the obvious.

"It's a nightmare I've dreamed about every night since I arrived here," I confessed to the dwarfs. "The very thought paralyzes me with fear. It doesn't make sense to do the opposite of what my subconscious is telling me except that my father once told me that the only way to conquer a fear is to face it. It may be a grave mistake, but I think I'll be haunted by the thought of what could have been if only I had tried. For Charming, I would risk my own life."

"Love sure is stupid," Glumdrops observed. The others nodded, and even I sighed in reluctant agreement.

"It sounds like your mind is made up, Princess," MisterMaster observed. "We won't try to stop you, but hope you'll return to visit us again."

"Of course!" I said, now realizing how much I would miss my new friends. I kissed each one on top of his head. Sillybird required a hug as well, and I noticed tears forming in his eyes. "I'll miss you most of all," I whispered in his ear.

The little men gathered their pickaxes and shovels and got ready to leave for work. At this point, Glumdrops began to protest my departure. "Snow White only found us by getting lost in the woods. She needs a guide to help her navigate the forest and make her way back into town."

"What a marvelous idea," MisterMaster concurred. "Thank you so much for volunteering to escort her!"

"Wait! I wasn't..." he interjected.

"You always pretend not to care, but you really are worried about the Princess," Grinny said with pride.

"I feel better knowing that she'll have someone looking after her," Slackjack added.

"But I didn't..."

"Come now, Crankypants," MisterMaster reasoned.   "Who else can do it?   I have to oversee our mining operation, Grinny will be cooking in Snow White's absence, Slackjack doesn't have the stamina to keep up with the Princess, Sillybird is nonverbal, which won't do as a guide, and Patches and Cruncher are our best gem cutters.   Plus, you know the surrounding vicinity better than any of us!"

"You're just making up excuses!" Glumdrops insisted.

"Oh, it's alright," I said with a smile.   "I'm sure I'll be just fine by myself."

"Oh, no you won't!" Glumdrops declared.   "I'm coming with you!" Everyone cheered, and Sillybird ran over to give him a hug.   "Okay, let's not get mushy now!   Gather your things and we'll be on our way."

"Thank you so much, Glumdrops!   I really appreciate your help!"   I packed us a basket with bread, meat and cheese.   I never had a chance to bake a pie, so I brought two apples as well.   Glumdrops grabbed his compass and a knife and was ready to begin our journey.

The other dwarfs headed towards the mine, while we started in the opposite direction after we waved "good-bye" to each other in an excessive manner.   I was very anxious to spend some one on one time with

Glumdrops.   I was kind to everyone I encountered and was uncomfortable when someone did not respond to me favorably.   Aside from the Queen, I'd not experienced such dislike before.   But unlike her, I trusted Glumdrops implicitly and knew he meant me no harm.   I hoped I could get him to change his opinion of me.

I was still wearing the shoes I had taken from the rickety cottage, but the soles were now quite worn and not the best for making such a lengthy trek.   What choice did I have but to wear them anyway?   It was still better than going barefooted.   I looked down at Glumdrop's boots and noticed they were not in very good condition either.

"When I marry my Prince Charming, I'm going to return to your cottage with new clothes and boots for all of you," I promised.

"Hmph.   Getting a little ahead of yourself, aren't you?" Glumdrops pointed out.   I blushed with embarrassment.   Perhaps it was improper to daydream aloud.

We followed the river southward for quite awhile when I started recognizing landmarks in the scenery.   I was so hungry and tired the last time I traveled through that I was surprised I recognized things such as an oak tree wrapped in ivy or a boulder shaped somewhat like a frog.   Then it occurred to me that we were not far from the worn down house.   I began to panic a bit as I realized that I was wearing the dress I took from that home, though the golden skirt now looked a dirty beige and the dark blue bodice was torn at the seams.   What if the owner was home and saw me wearing it?

"Why are you fidgeting with your hair?" Glumdrops asked.

"What?" I asked, not aware of how my nervousness was manifesting.

"What are you worrying about?" he clarified.

"I was just thinking that it might be dangerous for you to refer to me as "Princess" or "Snow White" while we're traveling.   Perhaps you should come up with a nickname for me."

"That's a good point," he agreed.   He stared at me for a moment and then decided, "Since your hair is so dark and your skin is so pale, I will call you Black Frost."

"I like that very much," I told him.

"Then why are you still twirling your hair around your finger?" he asked.

"Am I?" I inquired innocently.

"You most certainly are.   It's going to be a long day if you refuse to be honest with me," he declared.

"But I do like the name," I insisted.   "It's just that we're approaching a house where I borrowed some things without permission before I met all of you."   The confession poured from my lips before I could stop it.

"You mean you stole," he corrected me.

"Yes," I admitted.   "The owners were not at home, so I took some food and clothing."

"So you're afraid that if we meet someone nearby, they might recognize your dress and realize you're the thief," Glumdrops surmised.

"Yes," I said, humiliated by the truth.   Now that he knew I was a robber, he would have a valid reason not to like me.   I guess becoming his friend was going to prove more difficult than I originally thought.

"Well, you did what you had to at the time," he said in a voice that did not hint at disapproval.   "Let's reroute through the woods and meet up with the stream again further down."

"Glumdrops, I'm so sorry to cause such a detour," I said both apologetically and relieved at his understanding.

"What difference does it make as long as you reach your destination?" he shrugged.   Usually the slightest inconvenience made him grumpy.   I wondered why he was suddenly being so nice.

So we altered our course and headed into the dense forest.   The leaves were beginning to change color, which made the tree branches look as if they'd been set on fire.   I was grateful to have a companion to help me navigate the best way to go.

I wondered how the other dwarfs were doing.   They would probably have lunch soon and eat the remaining triberry muffins.   Sillybird might draw a picture in the dirt with a stick.   The others would laugh and take turns telling jokes.   I missed their constant chatter.

I was thinking these thoughts when a voice echoed through the trees, "Halt there, strangers!"   I froze at once.   A woman no older than myself with caramel colored hair and wearing a brown cloak walked towards us. She camouflaged into the foliage so well, it's no wonder we didn't spot her sooner.   In fact, if she hadn't spoken, we may have walked right past her and never noticed her at all.   "What business do you have here?" she asked when she was a few yards away.

"None," Glumdrops stated. "We are merely passing through."

"You've entered my circle," she cryptically said. "You must remain still until I permit you to continue on your way."

"And why exactly should we delay our journey?" Glumdrops asked in the annoyed tone in which I was accustomed.

"Watch and see little man," she promised. Just then a flock of geese flew overhead. The lady stepped back a few more yards and held both hands up to the sky. As the geese reached her location, she brought both hands down quickly, and the geese changed to a circular pattern and descended to the ground as if obeying her gesture. Then she interlocked her fingers together, squatted down and pushed her hands to the ground. It was as if a shockwave rumbled beneath the flock encircling her and all the birds instantly fell down dead. I had never witnessed anything so unnatural in all my life. I gasped in horror and surprise.

The woman grabbed a single goose by its feet and headed back to our location. "You may have this for the inconvenience I've caused you," she said as she offered us the carcass. My body trembled involuntarily. Immediately, I thought of the rickety house with the dead birds hanging from the ceiling. By trying to avoid its inhabitant, we were led straight to her. Would she figure out who I was?

"I'm afraid we have to refuse," Glumdrops spoke. "We have a long way to go and just want to keep moving."

"Suit yourself," she shrugged. I was still standing frozen in place staring at her intense green eyes as if they'd cast a spell on me.

"C'mon, Black Frost," Glumdrops urged.   "Let's be on our way."

"Black Frost?   What a precious name!" the stranger complimented me.

"Thank you," I managed to politely reply.

"You are a practitioner of the dark arts, I presume," she said.

"Oh, I'm not any kind of artist," I said, not understanding what she meant.

"Then how did you manage to enchant this dwarf?" she wondered.

"Hmph!   She's done no such thing!" exclaimed Glumdrops.

"Hasn't she, though?" she said to him with a smirk.   Glumdrops snorted.

"He's my friend," I tried to clarify.

"Well, you're a conspicuously odd looking couple," she informed us. "You must be in some sort of trouble that's forced you to travel together."

"It's none of your business," Glumdrops reminded her in an angry tone. "We'll be on our way."

"Sorry we interrupted your day," I said both impressed and fearful of the woman standing before me.

"There's no need to apologize, Black Frost," she assured me.   "I wish you and your companion a safe journey.   Come find me if you ever require my help."

"But you never told us your name," I said as Glumdrops led me by the hand away from the stranger.

"I go by many names," she called after us.   "You can call me Willow."

By now she was fading out of sight .   I saw her collecting the geese and putting them into a large sack.   I wondered what she would do with them, besides hang them from the ceiling.

We walked in silence for the next twenty minutes, and then Glumdrops finally erupted, "That woman was a witch!   Do you not understand that? She could have easily killed us both!   I do not intend to die on this journey! Be sure you never speak to her again!   Are you listening to me?"

"Yes, Glumdrops, I've heard every word.   There's no need for you to shout at me," I said now in tears from being reprimanded.

"Let's just hope the rest of our day remains uneventful," he said.

When we reached the stream again, we sat down and ate some of the food we had packed.   Glumdrops was eating hungrily when I glimpsed something shiny in the basket.   I quickly examined it and saw that it was a gold bracelet with a round charm, the size of a large coin, hanging off it. There was a picture of a tree etched in the charm on one side, while the other side was a small mirror.   It was beautiful, and I knew at once that it must have fallen from Willow's wrist and landed in our food basket when she was offering us the goose.   I was quite embarrassed to realize I had stolen from her again, albeit by accident this time.   I tucked it back into the basket, deciding that I could return it to her with a new dress and a basket of food someday in the future.   I would explain everything, and she would understand and forgive me.   Wouldn't she?

"What's a witch?" I asked Glumdrops as I bit into my apple.

"What!   You don't know?" he exclaimed in shock.   "You've led a sheltered life, Princess.   Witches use magick for their own personal gain. Some are believed to be wise, for they understand the flow of energy that controls everything in nature.   But many abuse this power and become wicked.   They use demonic forces to bring harm to others."

My eyes grew large with fright.   The memory of my time at Willow's house was still so vivid; it was a creepy place.   I remembered some bedtime stories my father had read to me about people using magick.   I thought magick was purely fictional until I saw those birds fall from the sky on command.   Perhaps, I would not return the bracelet to Willow after all.

Glumdrops watched the fear appear on my face and decided to change the subject.   "Maybe we should rest here for the night.   The sun will be setting soon."

"No!   There's no possible way that I can sleep tonight," I said.   "I'd rather keep moving; these woods make me uneasy.   Will you be able to navigate at night?"

"The moon is nearly full, so we're in luck," he assured me.   "Are you sure you're not too tired?   We've walked all day."

"I'm fine.   I'm ready to keep going."

And so we did.   My mind was racing with frightful visions.   In the black of night, the tree branches looked like shadowy hands grasping to grab me.   A distant fog appeared like ghostly apparitions coming to meet us.   Owls descended out of nowhere to catch their prey.   Just when I felt I could take no more, a trickle of light began to illuminate the sky.   Morning had arrived just as we entered the outskirts of the village.   The palace did not look so far away now.   Even though I knew I was not welcome, it stood there beckoning me home.

A Thousand Miles

"Cause you know I'd walk a thousand miles

if I could just see you   tonight." ~ Vanessa Carlton

I stained my lips and cheeks with berry juice before proceeding into town.   Glumdrops insisted I wear my shawl around my head to add to the disguise.   My hair was so disheveled that I didn't think it made a bit of difference.   My tattered dress alone was enough reason for people to overlook me as being their Princess.

"What Willow said is correct," Glumdrops admitted with disappointment.

"What is?" I asked in confusion.

"We stick out like a sore thumb," he stated.   "It might be better if we pretend not to be traveling together when we reach the village."

"I won't be able to sneak you into the palace anyway," I pointed out. "Maybe we should pick a place to meet after I retrieve the map."

"Are you going to be okay wandering the palace alone?" he asked with concern.

"I'll be fine," I assured him.   "I know where I have to go, what I have to do and exactly how to do it.   I just have to be sure to avoid the Queen."

"How long do you think it will take you?"

"Maybe an hour," I estimated, "two at the most."

"That will give me time to buy some food for the next leg of our trip," he decided. "I brought a few coins along, in case we needed them."

I reached into the basket and felt for the bracelet. I clasped my palm around it and then handed the basket to Glumdrops. "I'll meet you at the fountain in the town square when I'm done," I told him.

"That's fine, but when you see me, keep walking so no one knows that we're together. I'll follow behind you a short distance until we reach the edge of the forest," he decided.

"Then I'll be on my way," I said with confidence as I started towards the castle.

"Be careful, Black Frost," Glumdrops called after me.

I turned and smiled at him. "Don't worry about me!" Though I acted brave, I felt a little nervous strolling through town and kept my head down. When I was out of Glumdrops sight, I slipped the bracelet I was concealing onto my wrist.

At last, I reached the perimeter of the castle. I kept to the right and made my way to the backside of the palace. It took a rather long time to reach the correct spot, but finally, I found it. There stood an old oak tree that had limbs that extended far enough to slide down the wrought iron bars of the fencing surrounding this side of the palace grounds. I had never dared to sneak out of the castle, but noted its potential to myself one day when I was bored.

Climbing up the tree was difficult when my legs were so exhausted from walking, but somehow I managed.   As soon as I was on the other side of the fence, my adrenaline began to accelerate.   I was now in the orchard and had a ways to go before sneaking within the castle.   I made my way quickly, but carefully through the gardens carrying a bucket of ripe apples, in case anyone saw me.   I could always explain that I was bringing them to the kitchen to be pressed for cider.   The courtyard was busy, but no one seemed to pay attention to me.   They were probably preoccupied with their own tasks.

I made my way to the servants' entrance and headed straight to the laundry room.   Fortunately for me, no one was currently scrubbing the dirty clothes or hanging them out to dry.   So, I searched through a pile of freshly pressed women's uniforms and found one my size.   I quickly changed and discarded my dress in the trash.

Then I headed towards my old bedroom.   I couldn't resist the urge to see if the Queen had left it unchanged or if every last trace of me had been eradicated.   Though I didn't expect it, I hoped that some of my room still remained as it was.   I really wanted to hug some of my dolls "good-bye" as silly as that might seem.   But when I got to the door, it was locked.   What remained behind it was now anyone's guess.

I grabbed a broom from a cleaning closet and headed towards the Queen's study.   No one was inside when I peered my head through the door.   I went through some papers in the top drawer of her desk and eventually came across a map that looked current enough to be useful.

The kingdom I was looking for was called Starlightdorf.   There were also three gold coins and a comb that I put, along with the map, in my apron pocket.

I returned to the corridor and busied myself sweeping as two servants passed by me.   I eavesdropped on their conversation as they made their way down the hallway.

"No one knows where she's going.   She just asked that her horse be saddled and be made ready for an overnight journey," the first servant said.

"How many guards are accompanying her?" the second one inquired.

"That's the strange part - she insists on going alone," the first one clarified.

"That's too dangerous!   What if she never returns, like the Princess?"

"Do you want to tell the Queen she can't do something?"

"I'm not that crazy!"

"Nor am I!"

The two then disappeared into the library and could be heard no more. The Queen rarely left the confines of the palace, so I, too, wondered where she could be going.

Just then I saw her marching down the corridor.   The Queen looked exactly as I envisioned her in my dreams.   She was dressed all in black with her hair braided into a bun.   I pretended to be preoccupied with sweeping in order to avoid her glance.   All the same she paused right in front of me and demanded, "Help me with this at once!"   She handed me her cape, and my heart pounded so loudly I feared she would hear it as I clasped her cape in place.   She then continued towards the main staircase.   Thank heavens she was too self absorbed to notice me.

Even though I knew the Queen was leaving, I still felt nervous being in the palace.   It was a peculiar sensation of knowing where everything was, but no longer belonging to any of it.   Also, I knew Glumdrops was waiting for me.   So, I exited the palace, this time through the main gate and made my way back into town.

I saw Glumdrops waiting for me at the fountain with our basket replenished with food.   I made eye contact with him and then continued onward past the village and into the woods.   Once I was concealed by the foliage, I waited for the dwarf to join me.   His short legs couldn't cover as much ground as quickly as mine, and while I was waiting, I unintentionally fell asleep.

When I woke up, the sun was beginning to disappear on the horizon. Glumdrops was asleep at my feet.   I shook him awake and said, "Why did you let me nap?   Night will be descending soon!"

"We didn't sleep last night, so I decided not to disturb you.   Plus I was tired too!" he defended his decision.

"What if I had been poisoned at the castle?   You should have woken me up!" I maintained.

"You were breathing well enough," he rolled his eyes.   "We can travel by moonlight, like we did last night.   Let's look at the map and eat while there's still daylight."

I took the map out of my apron and spread it out for Glumdrops to see it. "It seems the huntsman was actually taking me in the correct direction. Charming's kingdom lies north of this one."

"It might take us close to a week to walk there," Glumdrops decided.

"We should be able to buy some supplies along the way. I managed to take these as well," I said as I showed off the gold coins.

Glumdrops began to chuckle. "You've really transformed from Snow White, the innocent Princess to Black Frost, accomplished thief." I wasn't sure if he meant this as a compliment or insult, so I blushed and said nothing.

We began eating cornbread and ham while deciding the best route to reach our destination. As we started walking again, I pulled out the comb, which was made of ivory, and began to work the tangles out of my hair. It was a painful process. I checked the small mirror on the bracelet to see if I was making any progress.

"You stole more items than I would have guessed," Glumdrops embarrassed me again.

"Only the comb was a luxury item," I defended myself. "The map and coins were completely necessary."

"You seem to have forgotten the bracelet," Glumdrops pointed out. I didn't bother to correct him. I knew that I was lying by omission, but was afraid that if he knew it belonged to a witch, he would toss it into the brush, leaving me without a mirror.

Traveling in the evening did not frighten me as much as it had the previous night. It seems that my father had been right - once you face a fear, it can no longer intimidate you the same way again.

"I saw the Queen today, but she failed to recognize me," I told Glumdrops.

"Are you sure she didn't know who you were?" he asked in alarm.

"I'm absolutely certain," I assured him. "I haven't seen myself in a mirror for quite some time and even I don't recognize myself anymore." I paused for a moment. "Maybe Charming won't either."

"Well, if he doesn't, he's a fool who doesn't deserve you anyway," declared Glumdrops. I smiled; maybe the dwarf liked me better than I originally thought.

After awhile, we stopped and slept some more, so we would not fall into a pattern of walking at night and sleeping during the day.

I was back in the orchard again, but now the trees were bare of fruit and leaves. The naked branches were covered in a veil of snow, and as the snowflakes danced in the air, I saw him approach.

"They told me you were dead," Charming spoke to me as if I were a ghost.

"Perhaps I was," I replied. "Without you near, I certainly did not feel alive."

"Maybe you are dead still," he said. "You may just be an apparition come to haunt me."

"Then resurrect me from the dead and make me real once more," I begged of him.

He leaned in to kiss me, but as soon as his soft lips brushed mine, he completely vanished.

I awoke to the sun pouring through the branches.   I was relieved to no longer be dreaming about the Queen, but was disappointed to leave Charming behind in my fantasies.   Still, I stretched and rose, reminding myself that every step I took was bringing me one step closer to him.

The days slipped by uneventfully.   I was able to bathe most of the berry stains and dirt away at a waterfall we found on our third day of travel. I hoped that washing and combing my hair would make me appear somewhat recognizable to Charming.   Our food supply dwindled quickly, and we relied heavily on fruit, berries and mushrooms for sustenance.

Eventually, we saw Prince Charming's palace come into view.   The castle was set so high upon a hill that it appeared as if it were floating on a cloud.   Residences were not built together in a village, but spread out over lots of land on individual farms and pastures.

We started to pass some of these homesteads when Glumdrops asked me what my plan was.   "I'll march straight to the castle's main gate and explain to them that I am the missing Princess from Whitebirchburg, and that I am seeking sanctuary from the Queen, my stepmother, who is trying to have me killed."

"Are you sure that's the best approach?   What if they don't believe you?" Glumdrops asked.

"Honesty is still the best policy," I decided.   "We'll see what happens when we get to that point."

Just then, a mole emerged from an underground tunnel and wandered over to Glumdrops.   He looked at the mole and saw that the number 7 had been painted upon its back.   His face turned green, and he said, "I'm sorry, Princess, but I have to leave you now.   There's a problem back at the cottage."

"What?" I said, completely in shock.   "How can you tell?"

"We're miners by profession and have trained a few moles to relay messages to one another.   If there's ever a cave in or other emergency, we send one to alert the others," he explained.   "We've each been designated a number.   This seven means that Sillybird is in trouble."

"What kind of trouble?" I asked, now worried for my silent friend.

"If they sent a mole, it has to be really serious.   He may be dying," Glumdrops said with a shiver.

"Oh my goodness!" I exclaimed as tears began to wet my cheeks.   The other dwarfs felt like brothers to me, but around Sillybird I felt more like a mother than a sister.   I was protective of him and wanted to fend off anything that might harm him.   "I'm going with you," I told Glumdrops.

"What?!   You can't!   We've come this far!   You're only about a day away from seeing your Prince!" Glumdrops reminded me.

"I know, but if anything happens to Sillybird, and I didn't get to see him again, I'd never forgive myself," I sobbed to Glumdrops.   It wasn't just a matter of choosing friendship over a possible romance.   As a substitute mother, I couldn't abandon my child.   I'd been acting selfishly, like a spoiled Princess.   Now I promised myself I would do whatever I could to save Sillybird.

"We have to move quickly," Glumdrops wrung his hands together in panic.

"We still have the gold coins; maybe we can barter them for a horse from a local farmer," I said.

"That's quick thinking, Princess," Glumdrops commended me.   "Let's hurry!"

We approached the nearest home and knocked on the door.   A man, in his thirties, opened the door and stared at us as if we were the strangest sight he'd ever encountered.

"Excuse us sir, but our friend is sick and we need to get to him as soon as possible.   Would you be willing to sell us a horse?"   Glumdrops spoke quickly.

He laughed as if he'd just been told a joke.   "I might, but you two don't look like you have any money."

"I have this," I said as I handed him two of the three gold coins.

"These are pure gold!" he said in disbelief.

"Do we have a deal?" Glumdrops asked.

"Yes," he said, still processing what was happening.

"Do you have a pen and inkwell that we can borrow as well?" I asked.

"I do," he said again with surprise.   "Can you write, Miss?"

"I can," I informed him, though I understood his confusion.   We truly did look like a pair of homeless vagabonds.   I handed the map to

Glumdrops and said, "Trace a route from this kingdom to your cottage."

He obliged.   Then I flipped the map over and on the back wrote:

To my Prince Charming,

My stepmother has tried to kill me, but I escaped.   I'm living with seven dwarfs in a cottage in the woods.   Please follow the map to find me. With a hopeful heart,

Snowdrop

"Please take this letter to the castle and insist that it be read by the King's only son," I instructed the stranger.

"Why should I?" he asked with apprehension.

"The Prince will reward you handsomely when you deliver it - that's why!" Glumdrops said, understanding that when money talked, this man listened.

"Your wish is my command," he told us.

A brown horse speckled with white was the chosen mare for the job. "Her name is Snowflake, which is perfect since your name is Snowdrop," the man informed us as he helped us on her back.

"And your name is?" I asked.

"Liam," he said.   He seemed embarrassed for admitting he read the letter, but as long as it reached Charming, I didn't care.

"Thank you for your help, Liam," I said to him.

"Fare thee well!" he responded.

And then we were off, retracing the direction we had come.   Each stride taking me farther from Charming as his castle began to disappear into the clouds.

Now I Can Die

"I've got more to give, you know I do, but if tomorrow my number should be called, I won't be sad, I won't feel bad at all." - Nina Gordon

Even as I held tight to Snowflake, everything seemed to be moving in slow motion. My head was full of worry, and I had nothing to do but think. I knew from experience that it was often dangerous to be alone with your own thoughts. I worried most about Sillybird and only occasionally of Charming, but for the first time in forever, I was not thinking of myself at all. I was suddenly embarrassed over how self absorbed I must have appeared to the dwarfs. Still, there was time to set things right, wasn't there? My heart was a confusing mixture of hope and fear. Silent tears spilled down my cheeks, and I was glad that Glumdrops rode behind me and could not see my face.

"Courage, Princess," he unexpectedly said to me. "You are brave enough to face whatever awaits us." How had he known that I needed those words of encouragement just at that moment? And soon enough, I realized why. The terrain around me began to look familiar, and I knew we would be home at the cottage in only a moment.

As the cottage came into view, I felt like I was in a daze. I must have gotten off Snowflake's back and stretched my stiff legs, but I don't remember actually doing so.   What I do recall is Glumdrops giving my hand a reassuring squeeze as we opened the door and went inside.

The house was quiet and there was no one in sight.   I wanted to speak, but the words would not come to my lips.   "We're home!" announced Glumdrops when I could not.

MisterMaster, alone, came down the stairs.   "Crankypants, thank goodness you got our message!   Princess, I didn't expect that you'd return to us too!"

"Never mind that now," I declared with urgency.   "Let us see, Sillybird!"

"Wait!" he ordered as he spread his arms, blocking our ascent of the staircase.   "I need to warn you of his condition, so you won't be in shock. He's bedridden and weak.   He's been suffering convulsions and vomiting blood for the past four days.   Nothing seems to make him any better, and he now looks like he is at death's door."

"Then out of our way, so we can see him!" Glumdrops demanded. MisterMaster stepped aside, and I followed Glumdrops up to Sillybird's bed.

The remaining dwarfs were keeping vigil at his side.   Though we'd been forewarned, I still let out an audible gasp of surprise when I saw the smallest dwarf.   He was sweating profusely and shaking.   Sillybird could not speak, of course, but was bellowing such loud, strange sounds that I knew he was in immense pain.

My feet became frozen, even though I wanted to comfort him. Glumdrops approached his side first and said, "Hmph!   Some folks will do anything for attention!" Sillybird managed to smile at his friend. Making a fuss was not Glumdrops' style, but I knew inside he was just as concerned as everyone else.

At last my feet began to move again and carried me over to his bed. "Oh, Sillybird! I missed you so much!" I hugged his small frame and kissed him on the cheek. "I can't wait for you to get better so we can pick apples and bake a pie. We'll have so much fun together, but now just rest and become well." He placed his head on my lap, and I held him like a mother comforting her sick child. I lulled him to sleep humming:

"An apple a day, can't keep me away,

Soon we will play is the wish that I pray."

All the while, I heard Glumdrops speaking in hushed tones to the other dwarfs. "What remedies have you tried?"

"He can't keep any food down, though we've tried giving him ginger broth and crushed peppermint," Cruncher reported.

"His fever won't go down either," added Patches.

"I'm not sure he will get better," Grinny sniffled.

"How did this happen?" Glumdrops demanded.

"We have no idea," admitted Slackjack.

"I sent him home from the mine early to gather berries for us to have with our supper," MisterMaster explained. "When the rest of us returned home, he was violently ill."

"Do you think he was bitten by something poisonous, like a snake or spider?" Glumdrops wondered.

"We checked him over for signs of a bite or infection and found none," Patches stated.

"Since Sillybird is nonverbal, we can only really guess," MisterMaster continued. "When we asked him what happened, he just shrugs. Yet, none of the rest of us have become ill, so at least, it doesn't appear to be contagious."

The dwarfs continued to talk about what could be done, but I was no longer listening. I was now just gazing at my tiny friend and praying for a miracle that I already understood was not going to come true.

I fell asleep at his side and when morning had broken, I knew that Sillybird was not long for this world. His breathing was labored, his face was pale and he looked at me with eyes that already appeared to be elsewhere.

MisterMaster wandered over to my side with something shiny in his hands. "Here," he said, handing me my crystal tiara. "Sillybird dug this up the day that you left us. He washed your gown and scrubbed this crown until it sparkled. We may have forgotten you were a Princess and treated you like our maid, but he never did. I'm sure he would be proud to see you wear it now."

"Thank you," I said as tears streamed from my eyes. I placed the tiara on my head, and Sillybird smiled at me with the largest grin I had ever seen. "I feel rich, not because I am of royal blood, but because I am blessed to have such wonderful friends," I confessed.

We all formed a semicircle around Sillybird's bed and held hands.

"It's time to feel no pain anymore, only love," MisterMaster solemnly promised him.

"Don't remain here for our sakes," Glumdrops sniffled. "You don't deserve to suffer like this. You led a happy, meaningful life. Peace awaits you on the other side, but our love will remain with you when you go, so don't be afraid."

By now, Sillybird's eyes had closed and his face became still. "I love you," I said to him as I kissed his forehead. His lips let out one last gasp, and he was gone from us forever.

I'd been deeply affected by death in my lifetime, but never experienced it first hand like this. Sillybird had died the same way he lived - surrounded by his caring family. I stayed by his side, sobbing for what must have been hours.

The other dwarfs came and went, no doubt making preparations for a burial. At one point, it was just Glumdrops by my side, and he said, "Sillybird was never like the rest of us. He was a human child, abandoned on our doorstep many years ago. I'm not sure if he was orphaned or simply unwanted because his growth was stunted and his voice was mute. But he belonged here and always made the best of every situation. With the right attitude, you can always fit it - even in places you were never meant to be."

"Why are you sharing all this with me?" I asked as my voice still trembled from crying.

"Because the two of you are not so different," he told me. "No

Princess belongs in the modest home of aging miners, but here you are. I know it's selfish, but I hope your Prince never comes for you."

"If I could bring Sillybird back, I'd wish my Prince away as well," I admitted. "But I know that death is final and not everything I want in life will be granted to me."

"Why don't you come outside and collect some flowers for the grave," Glumdrops suggested. I decided I had lingered at Sillybird's side for longer than I probably should have, so I nodded and made my way downstairs. It was then that I saw my purple gown folded upon the table. Since Sillybird had procured it for me, I decided it was only fitting that I wear it to his funeral. After I changed, I made my way outside.

I began gathering wildflowers as well as leaves that were golden, amber and crimson. I wandered further from the cottage, as I kept finding things to place on Sillybird's grave. First, I found a rock shaped like a heart and then three crow feathers that were a perfect contrast to the flowers and leaves. Satisfied that I had a beautiful bouquet, I decided to make my way back to the dwarfs.

I had been staring at the ground for so long, that I was startled when I looked up and saw an elderly woman standing just a few yards away from me. I jumped in surprise, but the woman did not seem offended.

"Come, child," she beckoned to me. "I have fine wares for sale - pretty ribbons and combs for your hair."

"I'm sorry, but I'm in need of no such things," I explained to the peddler woman.

"I didn't mean to frighten you, and will now be on my way," she said to me in a crackly voice.   "I understand there is a house nearby, do you know if anyone there is home?"

"Please don't disturb us!" I pleaded.   "We've just had a death in our family."

"My poor girl, I'm so very sorry for your loss," the old woman replied. "Please forgive my intrusion and take this for your trouble."   She placed her hand in her basket of wares and pulled out a shiny, perfect, red apple. Though apples are not my favorite, there was something irresistible about this one.   "You know what they say about apples, child, don't you? Apples are for wishing.   The redder the apple, the more likely your wish will come true."

"No, I've not heard that before," I answered, wondering if she was bluffing.

"Such silly nonsense, isn't it?" she sighed.   "Still, there's no harm in trying."

"This is the reddest apple I've ever seen," I said as I turned it over in my small hands.

"An apple so pristine does look like it could be made of magick," the crone agreed.

"So what do I have to do?" I asked with hesitation.

"Just make a wish from your heart and take a bite," the peddler informed me.

I stared at the apple and finally declared, " I wish that love was enough to bring the dead back to life." And I bit into the luscious apple. The inside was as white as the outside was red. The taste was so intense that a trickle of juice seeped from the corner of my lips. I knew that I needed to return to the dwarfs, but I suddenly felt dizzy and short of breath.

A look of horror must have appeared on my face, because the old peddler woman said to me, " That is the magick working, dear child. Now swallow, so your dream will come true."

I remember having a difficult time swallowing, and then everything turned black. My body collapsed beneath me and all became still. I saw nothing. I heard nothing. I felt nothing. And yet, still I tasted the sweet and sour flavor of the apple.

Misguided Ghosts

"I'm just one of those ghosts, traveling endlessly, don't need no roads,

In fact they follow me and we just go in circles."   -Hayley Williams

My eyes fluttered open, and I saw flakes of snow falling from the vast, grey sky.   Slowly they fell, but I did not feel it.   I remained laying on the ground, wondering why the snow did not feel cool and wet when it touched me.   I stayed still and watched it accumulate on my body.   It did not feel heavy.   The odd phenomenon had me mesmerized.   Softly, I hummed to myself, as the snow covered me like a blanket:

"If apples were wishes,

They'd taste more delicious.

Dreams come true would grow on branches,

And I would never take my chances.

Red and shiny and full of bliss,

An orb as sweet as love's first kiss.

No one would ever have to die,

No mournful tears shed in good-bye.

As harvest time's special guest,

I'd gather joy to keep me blessed.

If apples were dreams,

Then I'd be the Queen."

I was not aware that the snow had completely buried me until I felt a hand grasp mine and pull me to my feet.   The hand did not feel warm or cold, but it did feel solid.   The powdery snow was shaken off my clothes, but still I did not feel it.   Not having my sense of touch working properly was quite disorienting.   Perhaps that's why I held onto that hand so tightly.

For a moment, the snow blew so heavily that it distorted my vision, and I could not make out the person attached to that hand.   I continued to hold on tight, and it did not let me go.   Finally, the snow slowed down and fell gently once more.   Through the flakes, I saw a young woman not much older than myself.   I didn't recognize her, but there was something familiar about her.   Her skin was fair and her hair was long and dark.   Her eyes were large and piercing, as if they held the secrets of the universe.   Like me, she was dressed in a purple gown.

"Can you hear me?" she asked.   Her voice sounded of kindness.

"I can," I replied.   My own voice now sounded strange to my ears. "Who are you?" I asked the fair lady.

"My name is Pearl," she said.   "And yours is Snow."

"Yes," I responded in surprise.   "I'm Snow White."   I wondered how she knew who I was.

"Do you know why you're here?" she questioned me.

"I don't even know where I am!" I admitted.

"You're in a place where 'what' and 'where' and 'when' no longer matter," she informed me.

"But 'why' is still important?" I asked quizzically.

"Why is always important," she assured me. "Why is the reason we love and hate, cry or fight, survive or perish. Everything we say or do is because of why."

"That's true," I agreed. "Even when I don't know the reason why something is the way that it is, I am still motivated by it."

"So, Snow White, do you remember why you're here?" Pearl asked again.

"I think I'm here to find Sillybird," I decided.

"Keep your goal in mind while you're here or you risk becoming lost," she warned me.

"Won't you come with me?" I asked.

"I'm sorry, but I cannot stay," she said as she let go of my hand. "I was only allowed to come here to greet you and remind you of your purpose - the rest is up to you."

I felt as if I was suffocating when she released her grasp of me. "Please don't leave me here alone!" my voice quivered.

"I'm always with you, Snow," she assured me, "even when you can't see me." She placed her hands on my face and the touch made me feel linked to her once more. Then she embraced me and said, "When the time is right, we'll be together again. Until then, remain true to what your heart tells you."

Then she let go again and walked past me to a tree that I didn't realize stood behind me. She climbed the enormous snow covered branches with ease and ascended into the heavens.   A mist concealed the top of the tree, so before long, her form had disappeared from view.   I touched the bark of the tree, but I couldn't feel it.

When Pearl was gone, the snow ceased to fall.   I walked through the fresh powder, but left no footprints.   At the base of the tree, I spotted a rock shaped like a heart.   I'm not sure why the snow didn't cover the stone.   Curious about it, I lifted the rock which appeared smooth, but again I couldn't feel it.   Underneath the earth looked soft, so I began to dig with my fingers.   The dirt squished between my hands, but my fingers and nails remained clean.   At last, I saw something shiny below.   I picked it up and brushed off the mud to reveal a pewter coin with the picture of a ship on one side.   The backside had the inscription: Please Admit One.   I didn't know the significance of the coin, but decided I should keep it.   I placed it between my cleavage since I did not have a pocket to put it in.   I patted the dirt back in place and moved the heart shaped rock on top once more.

"Princess," a voice spoke to me from behind.   I was so startled, I gave a jump.   I turned around and was horrified to see the royal huntsman standing before me.   I gave a scream, but he dropped to his knees and with a look of repentance proclaimed, "I can't harm you hear, Princess - nor can the Queen."

"What are you doing here?   Why don't you leave me alone?" I demanded.

"I've come seeking your forgiveness, though I know I don't deserve it," he revealed.   "I should have chosen loyalty to you, the King's daughter, rather than the Queen.   It's really my fault that both of us are now here."

"Do you know where we are?" I asked him, still not able to sort out my confusion.

"You mean, you don't know?" he asked awkwardly, as if he was embarrassed to explain.

"The last thing I remember was eating an apple in the woods near the dwarfs' cottage," I spoke of the memory still so vivid in my mind.   "Then I suddenly found myself here."

"The apple must have been poisoned, Princess," the huntsman clarified.

"I see," I said at last understanding.   "The old peddler woman who gave me the apple was working for the Queen."

"Or more likely, the Queen, herself," the huntsman told me.   "She's a formidable witch who can steal faces with the same ease she takes young girls' hearts.   She was probably in disguise when you saw the old woman."

After being so careful, the Queen trapped me at a vulnerable moment. Then I began to wonder if she was cruel enough to be responsible for Sillybird's death just to distract me.   I knew that she was.   I suddenly felt guilty for involving the dwarfs in my plight.

My silence seemed to worry the huntsman.   "Princess, do you now understand where we are?"

"Yes," I said in a hushed tone.   "This is Death."   This explained why my senses were distorted.   I was no longer moving through the land of the living.

"We are no longer alive, but this is only a piece of Death," he tried to clarify. "There's a hereafter that lies beyond this realm. I'm trying to earn passage there."

"Ah, now I see why you are attempting to be kind to me - it is still for your own selfish gain," I decided.

"The only way that I can be granted access to eternity is to be forgiven by someone I have wronged," confessed he.

"So, it's really quite convenient for you that the Queen murdered me," I grumbled.

"If it's any consolation to you, she had me killed as well," he replied.

"I'm sorry, but I am not in a very forgiving mood. You tried to assault me, and I was poisoned by the Queen only because you failed to kill me first," I accused him.

The huntsman sighed and gazed at me as if my answer was expected. "It's too late to undo the past, but please know that I regret putting my confidence in the Queen and would rally the kingdom on your behalf if I had to do it all again."

"Actions speak louder than words," I reminded him. "I'm not naïve enough to believe you." I began to walk away.

"Where are you going?" he asked with what seemed to be genuine concern.

"I need to find Sillybird," I said with urgency. Pearl had cautioned me not to get sidetracked, and now I was worried that I'd been wasting time.

"Who?" he asked, not understanding.

"He's my friend," I spoke as I continued walking. "He lost his life because of my stepmother as well."

"Let me come with you, Princess," the huntsman insisted. "Tracking others is still my specialty. Please, let me help." I knew his reason was insincere and that he merely wanted an opportunity for me to change my mind about him. Nonetheless, I shrugged and allowed him to follow.

The landscape around me began to change. The snow had either melted or disappeared. Before I knew it, we were walking through a field of lavender. I couldn't smell its sweet fragrance, but its majestic color made me feel more joyful. In the middle of the field stood a well, and as I approached it, I realized it wasn't just any well, but the very one from the palace courtyard. I remembered the coin I had found earlier and pulled it out to toss into the well.

"Stop! Don't do that!" the huntsman screamed as he ran after me. "What do you think you're doing?"

"Making a wish," I told him. "If you drop a coin into a well, you double your chances of your wish coming true."

"But that's not just any coin!" he exclaimed. "That's your ticket to an eternity of peace."

"What do you mean?" I asked in bewilderment.

"There's a ship that departs from here and sails through the heavens to the great beyond, but you have to have the correct fare to board," he explained in exasperation. "If you found your admission, it means you're worthy of eternal happiness. I may never find what you nearly tossed away haplessly."

"I'm sorry; I didn't know," I reminded him.

"This purgatory is full of temptations to lead you astray," he informed me. "Just because things are not as they seemed in our former lives, does not mean that this is a land of magick. Wishing your friend back will not make it so."

"Then I will find another way," I assured him. I left the well and began walking once more. "Please join me so I won't make another critical error."

"Yes, Princess," he eagerly agreed.

The scenery shifted again and the lavender disappeared into a copse of oak trees in radiant autumn colors. "Time appears to be moving strangely...there was a winter storm when I first arrived, but here the leaves have only began to change."

"I don't believe that time as we know it exists here," the huntsman surmised.

"Oh my goodness!" I said in surprise and delight. "Look there! In the middle of those trees is a lake of chocolate pudding!"

"Too bad we can't taste it," the huntsman smiled.

"But how is it even possible?" I wondered. "You said that you knew for sure that we were not in a land of magick!"

"You still don't get it, do you?" he sighed. "Everything we see here isn't real. It's not magick - it just doesn't exist. See that acorn cap? If I blow it like a whistle, it will make no sound." He picked up the acorn cap to demonstrate, and sure enough, there was only silence.   "Now take hold of my hand, Princess." I did so, and just like with Pearl, it felt solid.   "You and I are what is real here.   Our life forces recognize one another and are acknowledged.   Everything else is illusion."

"This is why you don't want to be trapped here indefinitely - it's lonely and confusing," I deduced.

"It's more than disorienting - it's dangerous!" he warned me.   "The longer your consciousness wanders here, the more you lose yourself and forget who you were."

"Can a person vanish here altogether?" I worried.

"You and I will never be hungry again because we no longer have bodies requiring fuel.   And here before us stands a lake of chocolate.   I don't want to become as useless as a dessert that will never be eaten," the huntsman's eyes conveyed their sorrow to me.

"We must find Sillybird quickly!" I proclaimed.   I knew that a place such as this would leave him vulnerable.

Still grasping my hand the huntsman insisted I focus.   "Think about what Sillybird might imagine.   Instead of looking for him, let's see if we can bring him to us."

But I wasn't sure where the dwarf might envision himself.   Could it be the mine or the cottage?   And then I decided to take a chance and closed my eyes.   When I opened them, we were standing in an apple orchard.

"Start picking apples," I instructed the huntsman.

"More useless food?" he questioned.

"Apples nourish more than the stomach," I rationalized to myself as well as him.   "Apple picking is good for the soul.   I never got to bake Sillybird that pie I promised him.   If he's thinking of me, he might just look here."

And then as if on cue, some apples dropped from the branches above us and Sillybird's goofy grin gazed at me between the leaves.

"Sillybird!   You are here!" I laughed with delight.   I held my arms out as the smallest dwarf jumped into my embrace.   He felt more than solid; he felt like the embodiment of all the love in the world.

"Mama Snow, you found me!" Sillybird declared in a voice I could hear, although his lips didn't move.

"Sillybird, I can hear you!" I gasped with excitement.

"The boundaries of the flesh are not present here," the huntsman reminded me.

"I missed you so much!" I told my small friend.

"I missed you too!" Sillybird hugged me tightly.

"We'll stay together from now on," I assured him.   "The Queen tried to tear us apart, but she didn't succeed."   I placed him on the ground and took his hand.   "After we find your coin, we'll be able to stay together forever."

"You mean this?" Sillybird lifted his stocking cap to reveal the same pewter coin with a ship on it.

"Why, yes!" I exclaimed.

"I found it when I first arrived.   I thought it might taste like chocolate , but it didn't taste like anything! So, I spit it out and kept it under my hat." Sillybird explained in such a manner that made me chuckle.

"Why would it taste like chocolate?" the huntsman asked, confused. I knew that the answer didn't matter.

Then I realized that the huntsman must be frustrated to see us so willing to lose the object he'd been seeking in vain.

"We just need to find one more coin for the man who helped me find you, and then we can be on our way, Sillybird!" I said.

"No, Princess," the huntsman interjected. "There is no coin for me. You must board the ship as soon as possible. The longer you linger the greater your chance of becoming lost." And as he spoke, the orchard disappeared, and we now stood on the dock of an endless ocean. Enormous sails were being raised on a sturdy vessel. "Go now," the huntsman insisted. "You were both the victims of an evil plot. You've earned your places in the hereafter." Passengers with coins were already being admitted on board.

"I've decided that you really did have a change of heart," I told the huntsman. "I grant you forgiveness. Once you've been redeemed by someone you wronged, you can ascend to the next realm, right? We still have time to find your coin!" I told him.

"Princess, your father and mother are waiting for you. It may be too late for me," he said in despair.

"But Sillybird and I never would have found each other without you!" I shouted. "I never would have been able to navigate through this land at all!   I might have been swallowed up in that lake of pudding!   I'm sure you've earned your way.   If we just look for a moment…"   And then I turned around and was frozen in my tracks.   Behind the dock was a vast field of snowdrops.

"What is it, Princess?" the huntsman asked with concern.

Turning to Sillybird, I said, "Will you wait for me a little longer?"

"What do you mean?" Sillybird asked.

"I need you to board the boat without me.   I'll join you eventually…just not right now," I told him.

He looked at me with the saddest eyes and asked, "But why?"

"There's something important that I need to do first."

"If it's important to you, Mama Snow, and you promise to find me later, then I can wait," Sillybird relented.

"No, Princess!" the huntsman shouted.   "I warned you not to become distracted.   The only happiness waiting for you is on that ship!"

"I'm sorry, but you're wrong," I smiled confidently.   "Please take this and keep Sillybird company on your journey," I said as I gave him my coin. "We'll meet again, eventually," I promised as I kissed Sillybird's forehead.

I walked away as the huntsman continued his protests.   I made my way to the flower garden and sat down amidst the snowdrops.   In the distance, I watched the ship departing.   Sillybird waved to me and the huntsman stood by his side, still confused by my decision.   I knew that Sillybird understood my reason, even if the huntsman did not.

Maybe you think that I gave up my passage as a gesture of forgiveness so the huntsman would finally earn his way, but you would be wrong.   I stayed behind out of selfishness, not selflessness.   I knew that someday, Charming would arrive here.   I couldn't risk him becoming lost and never being reunited with him.   If he still thought of his Snowdrop, he would find me here waiting for him.   I knew that it would take awhile, but I had forever ahead of me.   I could wait.

Bring Me to Life

"Wake me up inside, call my name and save me from the dark, bid my blood

to run, before I come undone, save me from the nothing I've become."

~ Amy Lee

The ship carrying Sillybird had just vanished on the horizon as I thought about Charming.   Our tragic love story had come to an end before it could even begin.   Still, I waited for him, hoping we could find happiness in death that we could not achieve in life.

I had not been sitting among the snowdrops for very long when I suddenly felt myself blacking out.   I couldn't see anything, but I did hear some muffled voices.   How could I be passing out, if I was already dead?

Another moment passed and then my eyes opened and my vision was restored.   Someone was holding me in their arms, and I saw that that person was Charming.   I felt myself choking.   I saw the bite of apple I thought I had swallowed lying on the ground.   It must have gotten stuck in my throat, and I coughed it back up.   Charming patted my back and my body grew calmer.   Charming felt solid and warm as he held me.   Then I placed my hands on the ground and it felt solid as well, but cool and moist. I heard the birds chirping in the branches above while autumn colored leaves fell all around us.

"Snowdrop, can you hear me?" Charming asked. "Are you okay?"

"Yes," I replied in a shaky voice. "I think I'm alright."

That's when I noticed that the six dwarfs were surrounding me as they began to shout and cheer.

"Princess, you had us worried!" MisterMaster declared.

"You're all here!" I said in surprise. "That means I'm alive."

"Of course you are, darling," Charming assured me. "You were just choking and had passed out. When I arrived, the dwarfs were in a panic thinking you were dead, but thank heavens, that was not the case."

"But I was dead!" I reported to him. "I even saw Sillybird!"

"Princess, that must have been only a dream," Grinny informed me.

"Oh, no, it wasn't!" I insisted. "The royal huntsman helped me find him, and there was this ship that took them to paradise. If I had boarded the boat, you never would have been able to revive me."

"Snowdrop, I'm sure that it was all your vivid imagination allowing you to say farewell to your small friend," Charming smiled. I knew the truth, but decided not to dispute their opinion any further.

"I'm just so relieved to see you again!" I told Charming.

"I hurried here just as soon as I got your message," he said. "Your stepmother told me that you had died, and I was so distraught! I didn't think that I would ever be happy again. The moment your letter arrived, my heart grew hopeful once more. Thank goodness you are alive and well!"

"It was my wicked stepmother's doing," I explained.   "She disguised herself with witchcraft and tried to poison me with that apple.   She's responsible for killing Sillybird too."   I glanced at the apple, and the ground under it had grown brown and contaminated.   Cruncher quickly buried it so no forest animal would be tempted to eat it.

"This is all my fault!" Charming lamented.   "If I had believed you when you first warned me about the Queen, we could have fled to my kingdom that very night!"

"But then we never would have met Snow White!" Patches protested.

"And Sillybird would still be alive," I reminded him.

"Don't fool yourself, Princess," Glumdrops interjected.   "You were the best thing to happen in Sillybird's brief life.   I'm certain he doesn't regret his fate."   A tear slid down my cheek.

"Friends, I think it's time for us to pay our final respects to Sillybird," MisterMaster announced.   Charming carried his tiny body from the cottage and placed him in the newly carved coffin.   We all surrounded the casket and kneeled on the ground with our heads bowed in prayer.

"Rest peacefully, my friend," MisterMaster whispered.

"We'll miss you, buddy," Patches said.

"Things won't be the same without your sense of humor," added Grinny.

"We'll always remember how positive you remained in such a dark world," said Cruncher.

"You made work feel more like play," Slackjack recalled.

"You said so much without ever saying a word," Glumdrops said solemnly.

"Thank you for helping Snowdrop when she was alone and in need. I can tell how dear your friendship was to her, and I wish we could have met," Charming spoke.

"We already said our 'good-bye', but I swear I will keep my promise to you, Sillybird," I said through my tears.

The coffin was lowered into the ground, and the dwarfs grabbed their shovels to complete the burial. I placed the floral bouquet I had collected on top, and we all remained there in silence a while longer.

At last, several of the dwarfs went inside to prepare supper. Glumdrops wandered to my side and in a low voice said, "I just wanted you to know that I believe you, Princess."

"What?" I asked, not understanding his comment.

"That you saw Sillybird in the afterworld," he clarified. "I believe you. I'm glad that he's okay, and that you came back alive to us." I smiled warmly at him and gave his hand a squeeze. "I know I told you that I hoped your Prince never came for you, but the truth is, you deserve to be happy."

"Thank you, Glumdrops," I spoke softly. "I'll never be able to repay the kindness you have all shown me...but I will try." I felt relieved to know that someone believed what I had experienced when I was dead.

We shared a final meal with the dwarfs. The mood was somber without Sillybird's presence. Still, I was glad to be in their company at the end of such an emotional day.

After dishes were cleared and put away, Charming announced that it was time for us to depart.

"It's nearly dusk!" MisterMaster protested.   "Why don't you wait 'till morning?"

"Nightfall will disguise us," the Prince reminded them.   "It's best that we leave as soon as possible before the Queen realizes her plan failed."

I felt reluctant to leave, but knew that Charming was right.   Tears and embraces were shared.   "I love you all dearly," I told my friends.

"Don't worry, Snowdrop," Charming soothed me.   "You'll see each other again soon."

At last, we were on the back of Charming's horse returning to his kingdom.   The journey did not seem long this time with him beside me.

"Snowdrop, now that you're safe at my side, I feel like I can breathe again," Charming said as we rode through the thick forest.

"Did you miss me as much as I did you?" I asked timidly.

"Even more!" he declared.

"Impossible!" I retorted.   "You can't even imagine the things I did to try to find you again."

He smiled and said, "Then will you agree to stay in my kingdom forevermore and be my bride?"

"Nothing would make my heart happier," I told him as I squeezed his back.

Then he slowed the horse down from its gallop.   I moved from sitting behind Charming to maneuvering my way in front but facing him.   As my

legs entwined around him, he ran his fingers through my ebony hair.

"I love you, Snowdrop," Charming proclaimed.

"I love you, too," I promised him.   "Forever and always."

Then we shared our first real kiss.   It was sweet and tender, and

because we were on a horse, a little awkward as well.   Still, it felt meant to

be.   It was the precise moment that I knew I would never be alone again.

When we reached Starlightdorf and began ascending the hill to the

castle that stood at its crest, I could hardly believe that I had finally made it.

The closer we got, the palace looked less like a dream and more like a reality

that would soon be mine.

Eventually, we arrived at the precipice and were ushered inside the

palace.   Everywhere I looked was polished marble and fresh cut flowers.

The beauty of the fragrant chrysanthemums reminded me of how

disheveled I must have looked in contrast.   Still, Charming insisted that his

parents meet me immediately.

The Queen hurried to meet us in the foyer.   She hugged her son with

relief that he had returned safely.   He must have left so suddenly that his

parents were full of worry.

"Mother, I'd like to introduce you to Princess Snowdrop," he said

beaming with pride.   "I've brought her home to be my bride."   I blushed

embarrassed by my dirty dress and windblown hair.   Charming's mother,

however, threw her arms around me in approval.

"Welcome, daughter!" she greeted me with enthusiasm.   "I'm so glad to finally meet you!"   My eyes filled with tears that I tried to blink back, but ultimately could not.   "Are you alright?" she asked in alarm.

"I'm fine," I replied.   "I've just never had a woman call me daughter before, and I didn't realize how much it would mean to me.   I don't know why I'm crying when I'm so happy.   Please forgive me!"

"There's nothing to forgive," she smiled gently as tears formed in her eyes as well.   "I've been dreaming about meeting you since the day my son was born.   If he holds you precious enough to be his wife, then you are dear enough to be my daughter."

That's when I realized I wasn't just gaining a lifetime with Charming and a new home, but a family who loved and accepted me just as I was. Amidst the hugs and tears of joy, the King made his entrance.

"Darling, have you made this poor girl cry?" he asked, teasing his wife.

"I'm sorry...I just can't help it!" I said to him.

"Princess, you've been through more than any girl your age should be expected to endure," the King said sympathetically.   "Now you are safe and loved and shall be for all your remaining days."   His kindness made me miss my own father.   I opened my mouth, but couldn't find the words to speak.   He held me tenderly as I continued to weep.

"Come, Snowdrop," Charming finally took my hand.   "I'll show you to your room."   We went up several flights of stairs and reached a huge room with a large bay window overlooking the kingdom.   The view was gorgeous and there was so much light dancing about the room.   There was a canopy bed draped all in purple and a wardrobe full of gowns exactly my size.   An adjoining room had a bathtub of steaming water.   The Queen must have overseen the preparations for my arrival.   "Let me leave you so you can relax in your new surroundings," Charming said, surely eager to change and rest himself.

After a quick kiss, he left my side, and I wasted no time soaking in that inviting tub.   As I undressed, I noticed that I was no longer wearing the bracelet with the mirror charm.   It must have fallen off during the journey. I decided that it no longer mattered and forgot all about my desire to return it to its owner.   I washed the dirt and grime out of my hair and cleansed myself of the old life I was leaving behind.   Loneliness, disappointment and fear would soon vanish from my vocabulary.   When I emerged from the bathtub, I put on a crisp, white nightgown and crawled into the soft canopy bed and slept peacefully.

The days that followed moved in a blur of activity.   I was given a tour of the extensive palace grounds which included several gardens, a labyrinth, and a waterfall.   The palace staff busied themselves decorating the wing of the castle that would soon belong to Charming and me, while preparations for our wedding were rapidly being planned.

Living at such a high altitude, winter arrived early.   The clouds that surrounded the palace sprinkled enough snow to make it look like an ice sculpture.   The beauty of the season never looked so magnificent, making it the perfect setting for our winter wedding.

Meanwhile, relations with my kingdom had been maintained.   It seemed my stepmother remained unaware that I was alive and well.

Charming decided that the best way to remove her from her position as Queen was to invite her to our wedding and have her arrested when she made her arrival.   I was nervous of the prospect of her ruining our special day, but it really did seem the perfect opportunity to capture her, so we would no longer be living in fear of what she might do to us next.

The day the dwarfs arrived for the impending wedding, my heart grew jubilant.   I had a surprise for them that I hoped they would love.   After greeting each one with a kiss on the forehead, I took them to our newly furnished wing of the palace.   The last room we went in had six small beds and dressers just the perfect size for my friend.   A closet held all new clothes, jackets and boots tailored to their stature.

"You made a special room for us to stay in when we visit you?" MisterMaster asked in shock.

"Yes...but I was hoping it wouldn't just be for visits," I stated.

"What do you mean, Princess?" Slackjack inquired.

"I'd like you all to stay here at the palace with me," I told them.

"Hmph!" Glumdrops muttered.   "What use would a bunch of old men like us be here?"

"You would be my royal attendants," I explained.   "You could make jewelry, cultivate a garden and do whatever else you like.   I don't really care how you keep busy; I just want us all to be together again!"

"If you think that hard working men like us would just abandon our current lifestyle to live in a cushy place like this..." Glumdrops began.

"You'd be absolutely right!" MisterMaster interrupted.

"Hooray! We're moving into the palace!" added Grinny. Patches and Cruncher began to do a dance while Slackjack tested out his new bed. Glumdrops rolled his eyes when he realized no amount of protesting would change the consensus of the majority. I knew that in time, he too would come around and be as delighted as the five others.

The day of the wedding, I awoke to a frozen wonderland. The purity of snow seemed to bless our day with the simplicity of love. The marble columns of the palace were draped with evergreen branches, white bows and pine cones. The glow of embers lit the fire places keeping us as warm as our hearts on this blessed occasion.

I wore a gown of ivory satin to offset my fair complexion. There was an overlay of lace in a snowflake pattern with pearl beadwork. The veil cascaded past the length of my black hair, and I held a bouquet of beautiful snowdrops.

The ceremony was held on a balcony above the castle's main entrance. The entire kingdom stood below to watch the festivities, but all I saw when I looked around were the dancing clouds. Snow flurries floated through the air as we recited our sacred wedding vows. My heart was overwhelmed by the emotion of love surrounding me.

I felt tears forming in my eyes. I didn't dare to look at Charming at that moment or I knew I would be reduced to weeping. So, I averted my gaze to the six dwarfs. First, I glanced at MisterMaster and the expression on his face echoed mine. I knew that if I cried, he might too. Then I looked at Cruncher, and he also seemed worried that I would start to cry.

Then Slackjack, Grinny and Patches all mirrored my expression.   The only exception was Glumdrops, who rolled his eyes as if expecting me to have an emotional breakdown on this mushy, romantic occasion.   And that was all it took for me to regain my composure.   I was suddenly determined to prove to that cynical dwarf that I could remain pulled together for the rest of the day.

We exchanged rings and were officially pronounced husband and wife. We sealed our joined fate with a kiss as our guests cheered our union.

The celebration then moved to the ballroom where food was served, champagne was consumed, dancing commenced and an enormous tiered cake of butter cream decadence was displayed.   Laughter filled the room as the dwarfs performed a jig.   Everything tasted divine.   Music played late into the night as the stars outside sparkled all around us.   I danced with each dwarf, as well as my new father-in-law, but most importantly, I danced with Charming.   His eyes locked with mine in adoration as we glided across the ballroom oblivious to the guests watching our every move.

As it turned out, I never did see my stepmother again.   There was a rumor that she did attend the wedding , but slipped away before she was caught.   She did not return to Whitebirchburg as Queen.   Knowing that I was alive, must have motivated her to find exile somewhere else.   Another family was placed in power and the kingdom I had left behind began to thrive once more, much to my relief.

For awhile, I lived with constant dread that my stepmother would not be satisfied until she had killed me.   But as the days, months, and years passed by, I realized she held no power over me any longer.

My heart at last felt complete.   I wasn't naïve enough to believe that all my days from that point forward would be happy ones.   In fact, there would be many awful days that awaited us - the death of Charming's father, a fire that ravished a third of the castle, political strife with a neighboring land, and an attempted assassination on my husband that frightened me to the core of my being.   But even at the most terrible of times, Charming and I knew that our worst day together was still better than the best day apart. So, I came to learn that living happily ever after is a decision that's made, not something that just happens to you.

Of course, there were countless wonderful memories that sometimes made joy come easily.   First and foremost was the birth of our precious daughter, Star White.   She was the bright light of our lives whose smiles were contagious.   Being a mother helped me heal the emptiness of growing up without one.   The dwarfs made entertaining nannies, and Charming's parents were the proudest and most doting grandparents.

There was also great fun in watching the fireworks at each New Year's celebration, as well as the many other festivals and galas throughout the year.   But Charming and I most often found happiness in life's ordinary moments.   Swimming in the lagoon, watching a butterfly land on Glumdrop's head, eating freshly baked bread, and kissing Star's scraped knee to make her feel better all brought me inexplicable joy.   Even the pain of a bee sting made me rejoice because I was alive to experience it. There was just so much of life that I nearly missed out on!

This is why I chose to share the story of my past with you. When I look in your eyes, I can sense it all - the potential for adventure, the moments of solitude, the longing for romance, the deep bonds of friendship you hold so dear, and the wonder of where you belong in this bizarre world. You are still young and your story has yet to be written. I don't know the details, but I do know that it will be a tale of amusing comedy, drama, some inescapable tragedy, but most of all great love. Always remember, you are my beloved daughter and you will be blessed, for the apple has not fallen far from the tree.

Katie White

Real a Lie

"I am that kind, living blind, for a lie."   – Melissa Auf der Maur

Have you ever had a secret so disturbing that you felt the need to conceal the truth at any cost?   Have you ever lied to so many people that eventually you believed the lie yourself?   My life is a carefully structured web of secrets and deceit.   I've buried the truth so deeply within myself that sometimes even I'm convinced that it never happened at all.   Then other days, the memory of the truth is so vivid that I'm afraid everyone must see me for who I really am.   Keeping my secret life hidden has become a lifelong obsession.

Take my name for example - what is it?   The answer's simple - anything I wish you to believe it is.   I've had numerous aliases throughout the years. Raven. Opal. Marina. Bianca. But the name that unquestionably suits me best is Your Majesty.

When I first met the King, I told him my name was Lilith.   I chose it because at the time I was reading a book on ancient Sumeria and was fascinated by their most feared Goddess.   The King became smitten with me very quickly, and because his daughter was named Snow White, he affectionately called me Lily White.   This silly sweet name made my skin crawl, but as I already mentioned, my name doesn't matter.   Seducing the

King was a means to an end and therefore, I allowed him to call me whatever he desired.

You see, my ultimate goal was to gain as much control as I possibly could, and the way I best saw fit to obtain the most power was to become Queen.   I was willing to do whatever it took - marry a man I couldn't stand, endure his pesky daughter, or wear a smile when I actually wanted to scream.   The payoff was great enough to motivate my every move.

At this point, you might already hate me.   But given the circumstances, who's to say you wouldn't do the same?

My life wasn't always like this, naturally.   I think each person's history is full of turning points.   Usually within the course of one's life, at least one pivotal moment will stand out as so significant that it will forever be thought of in terms of before and after.

So who was I before my life unraveled, and I was forced to rebuild it with careful lies to mask the pain?   Truly my life was hardly different from anyone's.   I was living an ordinary existence of mediocrity, and I was content.   No, more than content, I was actually happy.

I was raised by my mother, who worked as a seamstress in the royal court of the kingdom of Whitebirchburg.   Her days were spent at the palace creating the most gorgeous garments for the royal family.   We lived in a cottage in the heart of the kingdom.   Every morning, I picked up fresh rolls from the bakery across the street, and we ate breakfast together and discussed the day ahead of us.   She was training me as her apprentice, so occasionally I was allowed to accompany her to the palace.   On those days,

I would imagine what it must have been like to live as royalty and have your every want and need met.   But then we would retire home at the end of the day, and as I snuggled into my warm bed, I found it impossible to believe that any member of the royal family could be any happier.

Perhaps, I should have known more sadness.   I was a girl growing up without a father.   To the general public, my mother would announce that my father was deceased; in fact, he was dead to her in the figurative sense. But with me, she was completely honest and never hid the fact that my father was very much alive and furthermore, living happily in another kingdom with a different family.   Apparently, my father had wanted a son so badly that he swore to leave if my mother bore him a daughter.   Lo and behold, I made my arrival in the world, and my father made good on his word.

Given the circumstances, my mother could have resented me, but it seemed quite the opposite - that she cherished me as a gift.   She did, however, have a rather low opinion of men, not that I blamed her.   But I also observed our friends and neighbors and realized that ours was a rare circumstance.   I did not believe it was right to automatically hate all men. As far as I was concerned, I thought my mother was lucky that I was a girl. It helped her be rid of my father sooner rather than later.

My mother thought it important that I learn a trade so I would never be forced to rely on a man.   It was this upbringing that made me the self reliant woman I am today.   I owe much to my mother, but didn't appreciate her fully until she was no longer alive.   But that's a story for another time.

When I was sixteen, there was a period of great celebration for the kingdom when the King chose his bride. She was a lovely princess, named Pearl, with porcelain skin and dark chestnut hair. My mother set about the business of creating the most extravagant wedding gown ever made. Obviously, I was the only one she trusted to help with such a task, and I remember getting to know the Princess during those dress fittings. She seemed timid, but kind, and although she was extremely introverted, she also laughed a lot. I remember pretending that I was her friend and not merely a servant to her.

As my mother and I put together the beadwork of that dress, my mind began to wander, and I daydreamed what it must be like to be the Princess. Everyone cheered at her arrival; they took note of what she wore and how she had her hair done. She was famous, beautiful, and truly seemed to be in love. She seemed to have it all, and I admired her as well, but part of me hated the attention she was bestowed. In retrospect, I realize that it was the first time in my life I was ever filled with envy, but it wouldn't be the last.

Many things took place over the next several years that changed the course of my life: the kingdom grieved when Princess Pearl died a year later during child birth, my mother and I had a falling out and parted ways, I met a pair of wise old women who taught me the ways of the dark arts, my mother passed away before we could reach a reconciliation, and eventually, I put into motion my plan to become Queen. But most importantly, it happened.   The thing that drove a wedge between my mother and me. The thing that shamed me so much that I no longer felt human.   The thing that made me pay a visit to my father.   The thing that made me grow determined to be the most powerful individual in the kingdom.   The thing that made me both a witch and a queen.

You want to know my secret?   Promise you won't tell a soul?   Well who do <u>you</u> think you are?   It is for me alone to know and you to discover, if you can.   After all, before you can know the truth, you have to know the lie.

Crave

"Now I need a substitute for the love that you gave,

now I just can't be saved, and there is no salvation for me."

- Martina Axen

You've heard my tale of "before", now let me explain the aftermath. Since being significantly traumatized as a young woman, I decided I would reinvent my life.   I was too ashamed to return home to my mother, so I began wandering the paths that lead away from the kingdom and into the dense forest surrounding it.   I will admit to not having a plan; at that point, I was merely in survival mode.   But even in my state of emotional disarray, fate seemed to be grasping my hand and leading the way.

Just as twilight was descending, I spotted a rugged cottage truly in the middle of nowhere.   I heard two female voices coming from within and decided to take a chance and see if they might share their supper with me. I'm not sure what made me brave enough to believe this might be possible, but before I could think it through, I was knocking on the oak door.

"Who goes there?" I heard the voices ask in unison.

"You don't know me.   I'm a traveler in need of shelter this evening.   I was wondering if you might be kind enough to help me in my time of need?"

I heard the voices whispering in hushed tones and then complete silence.   Just when I had waited long enough to believe they meant for me to walk away, the heavy door opened to reveal the worn faces of two older women peering at me with apprehension.

"You're not some peddler trying to sell us something completely useless like decorative combs for our hair, are you?" the shorter woman asked me.

"No, of course not," I replied.

The other one chuckled, saying, "I told you not to worry.   Come in! Come in!"   And as I was invited in, I nearly began to regret it, for their home had an odd stench and there were all sorts of dead birds hanging from the ceiling.   Bottles and jars lined musty shelves, and on the wall were scrawled circles and grids I did not understand.   I sat at the rickety table, now afraid of what they were cooking for supper over the fire.

"You look like you have a tale to tell," the shorter woman observed.

"I thank you for your hospitality, but prefer not to share my story," I said, hoping I didn't sound rude.

The two women glanced at each other with sly grins.   Their disheveled appearance along with the creepy ambiance of their home was making me feel more than a little uneasy.   So I attempted to make light conversation.

"So, what are your names?   Mine is..." I began, but was interrupted.

"Don't tell us," the taller woman interjected.   "We believe names are inconsequential.   We will call you what we like.   You may call us what you decide for yourself." I was too tired and hungry for riddles, but I must confess these two women were keeping me distracted from my previous problems.

"Dinner is served," the shorter one gleefully announced. I was starving and grateful for food, but when they set the plate in front of me, I paused. It smelled like pork, but looked disgusting, like some internal organs I wasn't sure to be edible. They sensed my hesitation.

"Shall we say grace?" I asked, stalling.

They shrugged. "If you insist," the shorter one answered. Both pairs of eyes gazed at me to begin.

I clasped my hands together and bowed my head. "Lord, bless these women who have prepared this meal you have bestowed upon us tonight. We thank you for the gifts of food and company. Amen."

"Amen," they repeated with a snicker that seemed less than sincere. They immediately began to eat, and I knew that I could no longer delay doing the same. I closed my eyes briefly and assured myself that I could do this.

I took the first bite and was surprised by how delicious it was. It was hot, moist, salty and juicy. Perhaps it was because I was so tremendously hungry, but it tasted like the best thing I had ever eaten. After that first bite, my appetite was uncontrollable, and I began scarfing my meal as if it would disappear if I didn't eat it at once. And vanish it did; before long, I had devoured it entirely. My hostesses looked at me incredulous at first, and then they began to laugh.

"She actually ate it; I didn't think she would!" the shorter one declared.

Upset by their ridicule, I announced, "It was quite delicious.   Thank you so much for sharing this meal with me."   This made the old women giggle all the more.

"Do you know what we just served you?   That was a boar's heart - strong meat for one as frail as you!"

"Who are you to call me frail?" I gasped in disbelief as I stared at their hunched over bodies and wrinkled faces.   And then the taller woman grasped my right wrist with unexpected forcefulness and pricked my index finger with a sharp carving knife.   She then put my finger to her lips and began to suck the gushing blood.   "What are you doing?" I screamed.

And there before my eyes, she began to transform into a beautiful girl about my own age with ginger hair and cinnamon lips.   "Sister, you've had enough!" the other one hissed, and she too brought her mouth to my finger and began to drink and transform.   She also grew young and lovely with caramel hair and moss green eyes.   When she was done, she bandaged my finger and declared, "You have eaten the boar's heart, and it has made you strong.   Your strength became our strength.   From this day forward, we shall call you Piggy!"

Considering what I had just witnessed, there was much that should be questioned and addressed, and yet I found myself blurting out, "You most certainly will not!"

"Oh, Piggy, don't be mad!   We mean it in the most affectionate way possible."

"If names are so inconsequential, I dub the two of you - Crazy and Ugly!"   The sisters began to laugh again, amused by my declaration.

Crazy, the tall, ginger haired girl stated, "That's fine by us!   We've been called worse by our own mother!"

Then Ugly chimed in, saying, "Do you really want to argue about names all night, Piggy?"

"Not really," I sighed.

"Is this the first time you've seen the black arts in practice, Piggy?" asked Crazy.

"You already know it is," I sputtered in a disgusted tone.

"So, what shall we do with you?   Now that you've restored our youth, what use do we have for you?" Ugly pondered.

Suddenly, I was overcome with panic.   I had no doubt that these sisters could kill me in an instant with their witchcraft.   I was raised in a Christian household and taught that black magick was the devil's handiwork. These women were evil, and a I needed to get away quickly.

"Oh, Piggy, never you mind her; my sister is merely teasing.   Anyone who can stomach a boar's heart is a powerful ally to us," Crazy explained in a reassuring voice.

"Whatever do you mean?" I queried.

"Hold out your palm," Crazy instructed and I obeyed.   She traced some of the lines with her long fingernail.   "Your life will be one of turmoil, but you are full of creativity and a power not even you understand."

Then Ugly took out a crystal pendant on a string and held it over my open palm.   It took on a strange purple glow.   Ugly let out a gasp of surprise, and the two sisters stared at each other in disbelief.   Ugly muttered, "It's true; she has charisma and ruthlessness - she just doesn't know it yet.   With us to help mold her talents, we might become unstoppable."

Although I was frightened, I now sensed that I was in a position with more leverage than I previously realized.   Remember, I had no plan for my future, no idea where I would sleep that night, no clue where I would head upon leaving these women.   Perhaps if they saw some value in me staying, I could use their hospitality to my advantage while I formulated my next move.

Both women stared at me with hungry eyes as if deciding something I couldn't comprehend.   Again, I grew uneasy.

"I can cook and clean and mend clothing," I suddenly blurted out.   "If you expect me to stay, I will earn my keep."

The two burst out in silly laughter once more.   "You want to stay with us, Piggy?" asked Crazy.

"I do," I decided.   It was time to make a bold choice and see if it might pay off.   Plus, even if I were to die at the hands of these transformed hags, it might be a welcome respite from my miserable life.

"Then we will allow you to stay," Crazy said.

"For now," Ugly added.

"Welcome to the coven," Crazy joked as she put an arm around me and both sisters let loose their high pitch laughter yet again.

Suddenly, I grew incredibly exhausted and nearly passed out on the spot. The witches got out some quilts and a pillow and fixed a place for me to sleep on the floor. As I drifted off, I wondered if they had placed a spell on me or if I was just drained from all I had witnessed. I suppose the boar's heart could have contained magick, as well. Regardless of the factor, I was tired, but also frightened that I might not awaken in the morning. Despite my fears, fatigue overcame me and I fell into a deep, but disturbed sleep.

I awoke in the morning to a high pitched scream. I looked around the cluttered room in a panic, at first not remembering where I was. Then I heard the sound of footsteps racing down the rickety staircase and saw Ugly burst into the room.

"You!" she screamed in an accusing tone while pointing her bony index finger at me. "You did this to me!" She tugged at her caramel colored hair that I now realized was streaked with patches of gray.

Before I could respond, Crazy was at her side. "Sister, what's wrong?" she asked and then gasped, "Look at you!"

"Look at me? Look at yourself!" snapped Ugly and then I noticed she had a handheld mirror in her other palm. As Crazy glanced at her reflection, her face contorted in horror.

"Piggy, you lied to us - you're not a virgin!" Crazy accused.

"I never claimed to be!" I retorted as my face began to burn with embarrassment.

"Damn it!" Ugly shouted. "We just assumed…"

"No wedding ring, so pure in appearance - how could we have guessed otherwise?" Crazy grumbled.

I sat there on the floor, a mixture of anger, frustration and shame. I didn't dare speak a word.

"Only the blood of a virgin can restore our youth permanently," Crazy explained.

"But I thought you said last night that it was because I ate the boar's heart," was my annoyed response.

The sisters sighed, as if explaining things to an infant. "The boar's heart allows the transformation to take place, but it's virginity that gives the spell longevity."

"So you were specifically waiting for a young maiden to come knocking on your door?" I wondered.

"Don't be ridiculous," Ugly hissed. "How often do you think we get visitors? We have a bit of a reputation in these parts."

"We leave alone those who leave us alone," added Crazy. "We were merely taking advantage of a an opportunity that presented itself."

Ugly was still staring at me with a look of anger and disgust. "And so it didn't work out," I said. "You're no worse off than you were before I arrived."

Within a split second, Ugly had lunged at me with full force. Her long fingernails were clawing at my face and tugging at my hair. I screamed at first in surprise, then in agony.

"Let go of her!" Crazy ordered.

"Why should I?" Ugly demanded. "We've agreed to take her in, teach her our way of life and what do we get in return? If there is no payoff, then she should leave and not darken our doorstep any longer!"

"Enough!" shouted Crazy. "She may still serve her purpose, and you know it."

Ugly finally let go and walked over to her sister's side. She leaned on Crazy's shoulder and began to sob. "But I want to be pretty again! It's the only thing I really want!" she wailed.

"Hush, little sister. One day you will be. We both will," Crazy assured her, as she kissed her creased forehead.

After the scratches and bruises I had just received, I should have remained silent. I knew that I should, but I didn't, and the following conversation would haunt me ever since.

"But why does it matter?" I needed to know. "What purpose does beauty serve? It won't save you from unfair circumstances. It won't make you any richer, wiser or happier. We all grow old; it happens to everyone. So why do you care so much?"

Both women stared at me as if I couldn't possibly be serious.

"Beauty is everything," Ugly spoke. "Beauty is power!"

"Being beautiful won't solve every problem, but being pretty certainly takes you more places," Crazy added. "People judge instantaneously, and being pretty gives you an advantage."

"That's preposterous!" I maintained. "If your personality is ugly, no one will care how gorgeous your exterior may be."

"They will provided you're a good enough actress," Ugly pointed out.

"What matters to you more than beauty?" Crazy asked me completely serious.

"So many things!" I retorted. "Happiness, love, family, friends, inner peace..."

"And beauty can be a way to get all those things!" Ugly interjected.

"What about Princess Pearl?" I finally exclaimed in exasperation. "She was gorgeous, but still died in childbirth. Clearly, beauty is no substitute for good health!"

"Obviously, beauty can't save you from every circumstance, but it still helped her. She did marry the King despite her poor health," Ugly said as she crossed her arms.

"Beauty didn't get her that - her status did! She was born a Princess," was my rebuttal.

"But one can buy status when one has beauty," Ugly maintained.

I sighed, knowing that neither of us would concede to the other's point of view.

"Shall we make a wager?" Crazy asked in an enticing voice. Suddenly, I was reminded that these were not merely two silly sisters, but rather two well practiced witches.

"What kind of a wager?" I asked cautiously.

"If we convince you that beauty opens doors that are currently closed to you, you will help us regain eternal youth and be pretty once more."

"And if I cannot be convinced, you shall give me the money I require to continue on my journey from here," I said satisfied that they would not win.

"Our timeframe shall be one year," Crazy declared.

"Why so long?" I mused.

"We have much still to teach you before you will be ready to proceed."

"Then let's begin!" I stated with eager anticipation.

"Perfect," said Crazy. "Then tell me, what do you desire more than anything else?"

I didn't even pause. "Control. Circumstances beyond my control have torn my world apart. I want to feel that I have total control."

"Excellent!" Crazy exclaimed. "Control is the door that beauty will open for you." She smiled at me with such assurance that the hair on my arm stood on end. I suddenly realized that I wanted them to be right. I wanted their experiment to succeed and to have the control I craved granted to me.

Thus began my descent into the occult. I would learn magick and deceit and hone it like a fine art. These lonely, old women saw me as their pet project. I came to discover that having me believe their point of view would restore their belief as well.

The year went by quickly and everyday I woke up wondering, would beauty grant me the power I was seeking?

Any Day Now

"Any day now my destiny will begin, and until then I'll just be wasting my time. But don't you worry, I'll be just fine." – Bif Naked

I won't bore you with the details of that year spent with Crazy and Ugly. Suffice it to say, I learned the principles of nature and manipulation, discovered herbs and roots for healing, memorized incantations, found out what spells worked best according to the phases of the moon, uncovered the mysterious properties of crystals, unraveled the power of fire and water, and ultimately realized how grateful I was to grow up an only child! The sisters drove me mad with their constant bickering, and I lived for the moments I could be alone to practice witchcraft in a solitary manner.

Although the sisters were wise in the ways of sorcery, not everything they taught me seemed to have merit. I didn't understand the point of sacrificing a chicken to make our hair grow quicker. To make it rain or even prevent a frost might have been reasonable, but who is so vain that they slaughter an animal in ritual as part of their beauty regime rather than their dinner preparation? Obviously, I still didn't believe that being beautiful was the key to everything, but Crazy and Ugly were preparing me for things to come nonetheless.

At the ten month mark, I was put to a test.   "If you travel half a day, following the stream beyond the rock wall, you'll come to a small cottage inhabited by half a dozen little men.   They spend their day mining precious gemstones that they craft into jewelry to sell in town on certain market days.   As you know, a witch can be quite powerful with the right minerals in her possession.   Find the gems that you most desire and have them give them to you."   Crazy explained the goal in simple terms, but I could not follow the execution of her plan.

"What shall I barter with them?" I asked, sure that I was missing something important.

Ugly snickered, "You're not going to trade with them; that would be pointless!"

"Then I'm supposed to steal the gemstones?" I inquired.

"What kind of witch lowers her standards to that of a common thief?" Ugly said insulted.

"If I'm not stealing or buying the gems, then how do I obtain them?" I asked, outright confused.

Crazy sighed in irritation.   "Just as I told you - have them give them to you."

"What would motivate them to simply give me something that they normally sell for a profit?" I asked again, frustrated.

"They'll do it because you're pretty!" Ugly shouted, baffled by my obliviousness.

"That's the whole point, Piggy!"   Crazy said in exasperation.   "When you're pretty, things are handed to you.   This is the moment for which we've been training you!   You must believe in the power of your own beauty."

It was true that the sisters had been spending ample time improving my appearance.   I always thought I looked quite ordinary.   Since spending time with Crazy and Ugly, my hair had grown soft, shiny and strong, my skin was smooth and the complexion was peaches and cream, my lips were luscious and rose colored, and my figure was slim, but curvy.   We had pots of rouge and eye make-up that we concocted from various plants.   When my hair was arranged in an ornate braid, my face painted on, my bodice corseted, and I was wearing a silken gown, I really did look quite glamorous. Though my exterior looked up to the task at hand, inside I still felt nervous and insecure.

"Are you certain I'm ready for this?"

"How much time do you need?" Ugly wondered aloud.   "If you had come to us pregnant, you would've had the baby by now.   There's only so much preparation you can have before being thrust into life changing circumstances."

Ugly's words stung me with their truth.   It was time to take a chance and move forward.   I was strong and beautiful, and it was time for my new life to begin.

"I'll return tomorrow with the gems," I promised.

"We'll see you then, Piggy!" Crazy proclaimed.

"Don't fail us!" Ugly said with less confidence in me.

"Failure is not an option," I assured her and left.

Perhaps under regular circumstances, it would have taken a half day to walk to this cottage, but wearing heeled boots and a tight corset slowed me down quite a bit.   When I started on my journey, I felt gorgeous and powerful, but before very long, I felt breathless, my hair was sweaty and my dress seemed heavy.   I was losing confidence to complete my mission with every step I took.   By the time the cottage came into view, I knew I needed to collect my thoughts.   I leaned over the stream to splash some cool water on my warm brow when I saw it for the first time that day - my reflection.   I really was beautiful; so beautiful, in fact, that at first I didn't recognize it as me.   I turned quickly to see if some other maiden was standing behind me and then glanced back at my reflection.   All at once, I started to believe that the sisters might be right - being pretty might be all I needed to make this work.

I saw smoke coming from the chimney and surmised that the little men must be home cooking their supper.   I mustered up my courage and knocked on the wooden door of the cottage.   The door swung open, and I heard a voice ask, "Can we help you, Miss?"   At first, I saw no one there and then I glanced down and noticed a small, bearded man standing in the doorway.   I'd never seen a dwarf before and no longer felt at ease.   How could I use looks to my advantage with a group of men who lived simple lives without worrying about outward appearances?

"Yes," I answered the dwarf hesitantly.   "I was running an errand for my sisters and seem to have lost my way.   I thought perhaps you could help me."

"We can try," he replied with a friendly smile.

"Well, I heard a rumor that there is a place nearby where one might find precious gemstones.   My sisters and I each promised our mother to find her one for her birthday celebration tomorrow.   I was to find a ruby. My older sister is to bring an emerald, and my younger sister needs a sapphire," I said as the lies came easily to my rosy lips.   "I thought if I could find the spot containing these gems, I could help us all."

A group of dwarfs had now joined the first one I had met.   All of them had graying beards and patched, worn clothing.   The one I was speaking to was rubbing his hands nervously.   "I'm sorry, Miss, but the mine you're speaking of is property belonging to us.   It's too dangerous to allow just anyone to wander there."

"Oh, I'm so embarrassed!" I fibbed.   "Of course, I'd never try to steal!"

"No, of course not!" the dwarf assured me.   "I didn't mean to imply that you would; I certainly hope I didn't offend you."

"Why don't you invite her in for supper?" another dwarf offered.   "It's late and surely, she's hungry."

"Oh, I am a bit famished, but I've already imposed on you tonight and should be going," I said, hoping they would call my bluff.   I was certain that if I got inside their home, I could charm them into giving me the gemstones.

"Please don't go!   It's the least we can do after disappointing you," another one insisted.

"Well, if you truly don't mind...dinner does smell delicious."   Just like that I was through the door with my game face intact.

"Aw, shucks.   It's nothing special," said the dwarf who was cooking. "It's just rabbit stew with vegetables from our garden."   Truth be told, I thought the meal smelled wretched, far worse than eating a boar's heart. Still, I wore a permanent grin and played the part of guest of honor.   I took my seat at their low, long table and waited for the meal to begin.   There was no grace or passing of food; it just became a free for all of short arms grabbing what they could.   In the commotion, no one seemed to notice that I was hardly eating the foul meal.

"So, young lady," one of the dwarfs finally asked, "What is your name?"

"Madelynne," I said without pause.   "What are your names?" I asked out of politeness rather than genuine interest.

"Oh, dwarfs can't reveal their names to anyone," one of them answered humbly.   "We each have one true name that we keep secret. That way, no one can mock or dishonor us."

"But then what do you call each other?" I questioned in bewilderment.

"Nicknames....though, we all have several," another one confessed. "You can call us whatever you like."   This notion of inconsequential names was becoming redundant, but since I, too, was lying about mine, I decided I had no right to judge.

As the meal concluded, I thanked the little men for their hospitality and stood up as if leaving.   "Do you have to go so soon?"   I was asked.

"Well, I wouldn't mind seeing some of your gems before I go."   They were all too eager to comply.

"We just polished these this week," one of them proudly announced as he brought over a tray of glittering, vibrant stones.

"Oh, they're so beautiful!" I gushed as I held them up individually to examine them.   If I had wanted to, I could have grabbed the gems and ran. Even in heeled boots and a corset, I knew I could outrun the dwarfs' short legs.   But that would defeat my real purpose, so I sighed dramatically and handed them back.   "If only I could afford to buy these from you, I would!" I was learning that it took discipline and patience to maintain a charade, instead of being direct and gaining instant gratification.   It was much harder work to be nice than mean.

"Oh, we can give you a generous discount," one of the dwarfs replied.

"I'm afraid I don't have any money," I said sadly.

"Well, maybe you could clean our house and mend some shirts for us," another suggested.

"I don't have the time.   I really must be returning home before sunset," I said as I rose to exit.

"Come visit us anytime you're nearby," one of them said cheerfully.

"Of course," I smiled.   "And thank you again for supper."   The dwarfs all rushed to the door to see me off.   We waved good-bye, and I turned to leave, contemplating my next move.   I would feign an injury and be forced to spend the night.   They would feel so badly, they would eventually offer the gems as a get well gift.   But before I could trip over my own boots and begin phase two of my deception of the dwarfs, I felt a tug at the skirt of my dress.   I turned and saw a timid dwarf I hadn't noticed before.   He was the only one without a beard.   While the other six dwarfs had their backs turned, returning to the cottage, this one handed me a velvet pouch.   I glanced inside and saw three stones - one green, one blue and one red.   He put a finger to his lips, and I quickly placed the bag in the bodice of my dress.

"Our secret," I assured him as he gave me a silly grin.   Then he raced to join the others inside, and I began my journey back to the sisters.

Night descended quickly, but I had flint with me and made a torch to light my way home.   I removed the boots to speed me on my way.   I reached the doorstep before sunrise.   The sisters were still asleep, but Crazy wandered downstairs when she heard me arrive.

"How did it go?" she asked quietly, so she wouldn't disturb Ugly.

"It was a success," I proclaimed as I removed the velvet sack from my dress.

"Nicely done," she approved as she examined the three stones.   "Did you enjoy it?"

"At first, I found it frustrating to wait to be given something I could have easily taken, but I do see the merit of it.   Those little men adore me despite my intentions to swindle them."

Crazy smiled wickedly.   "Do you think you're ready for the real thing?"

"Who will I be deceiving?" I asked.

"The King," she answered.

Shivers ran down my spine.   To play games with dwarfs was one thing, but if I were caught lying to the King, I would lose my life.

"We need to plan this very carefully, there isn't room for error," I told Crazy.

"We'll discuss it more after you've rested," she assured me.   She helped me out of my gown and corset, then slipped back upstairs.   I crawled under my quilt exhausted from the day.   I should have been able to fall asleep quickly except that my mind was now racing.   Deceiving a King was not a matter to take lightly.   Part of me contemplated running away from these witches.   But where would I go?   The other part of me was curious about their plan.   I'd been in the palace before, perhaps I could use this to my advantage.   As I thought up a hundred different scenarios, I finally drifted to sleep.   I only know I slept because late in the morning I heard Ugly making a commotion in the kitchen.   I sat up groggy and gave her a hateful stare.

"Hey, sleepyhead, it's about time you woke up," Ugly said in a catty tone.

"Don't tease her," Crazy warned her sister.

Naturally, this encouraged her to taunt me even more.   "Wow!   Look at the dark circles under your eyes.   Maybe you're the one we should be calling Ugly!"

I was not in the mood for her attitude.   "Maybe we should trade...after all, you've grown fat enough to deserve the title of Piggy!"

Ugly let out a hiss, but Crazy interrupted by shouting, "Enough!   Today we have much to discuss."

"Yes, let's talk about the task at hand," I insisted.

"Piggy has informed us that her ultimate goal is control over her life. I don't see a better way for her to gain such power than by becoming Queen of this land."

"Queen," I repeated in awe. It was a role I never envisioned for myself, but now I was drunk with longing.

Ugly chuckled with disgust. "Piggy could never pull it off!" she exclaimed to her sister. Then to me, she said, "I never thought you'd agree to something so dangerous. You do realize that if your lies come unraveled, you'll hang for your crime."

"I understand," I said in a surprisingly calm manner. "But that won't happen because Crazy has a plan that cannot fail."

"Your confidence flatters me," Crazy stated. "Still, it is a risky matter."

"Too risky!" Ugly snapped. "If she gets caught, she'll sell us out! They'll burn us at the stake!"

"If I get caught, I promise not to take you down with me," I swore.

"We can't trust her!" Ugly pronounced to her sister. "Make her take an oath!"

"Very well," Crazy sighed. "Piggy, will you take an oath that all moves you make from this day forward are your own and that we hold no responsibility?"

"Anything to put Ugly at ease," I replied a little bitterly. The lack of trust was insulting, yet another reason I yearned to be in control.

"Lift up your skirt," Crazy instructed.

Even though I'd grown accustomed to the bizarre behavior of the witches, I still had moments of apprehension. "Why? What do you plan to do?"

"Just do what you're told," Ugly demanded. So I gathered my skirt up to my hips and waited with a sigh. "I'll hold her down," Ugly told Crazy as she wrapped her arms around me with such strength that I could not break free if I had wanted. Then Crazy came at me with a sharp dagger and my heart began pounding rapidly. I shut my eyes tight as she proceeded to carve a pentagram into my left thigh. I let out a shriek of pain, but she was done quickly, and Ugly released me when she finished.

"You have been scarred by the witches' seal. Every time you see it, let it be a reminder that your loyalty is to your sister witches and that you made an oath not to betray us," Crazy explained.

"I was right about you- you really are crazy!" I said in revulsion as I watched the blood leak from my wound and trickle down my leg. I could not wait to be acting on my own, even if the mission carried a chance of dying. I needed control and craved power. I had obtained beauty, witchcraft and the ability to successfully lie to others. These would be my tools to creating a new life for myself. I turned to the sisters and said, "I gave you my word, now let's begin!"

Beautiful Liar

"Let's not kill the karma, let's not start a fight,

It's not worth the drama for a beautiful liar."   - Beyonce Knowles

It took weeks of preparation to set things in motion, but I was now well on my way to tricking the King into making me his new bride.   I assumed an alias, Princess Lilith Worthington, of a foreign kingdom that doesn't actually exist.   I started to correspond with the King through a series of letters.   I layered on the flattery by explaining how well loved and respected he was in our kingdom as a just and kind ruler of his people. This hooked him enough to respond with a polite letter of his own.   Then we upped the ante by sending him a small portrait of myself.   It turned out that Crazy was actually a rather talented artist, and when the King received the picture of such a fair beauty, he invited me to be his guest at the palace anytime I chose.   When we received that letter of invitation, Crazy, Ugly and I laughed and danced, thrilled by our success.   It was all too easy, and I decided that Princess Pearl must have been rolling over in her grave at her pathetic husband's naiveté.

We forged the necessary paperwork to prove I was of royal lineage. My seamstress skills came in handy when I constructed a wardrobe of elegant gowns befitting a princess.   Crazy welded a necklace with the gems I'd been given by the dwarf.   Ugly stole two horses, though I wasn't sure of the details of how that was accomplished.   Crazy came up with a sympathetic back story that was sure to win over the King.   We sent a letter announcing my impending arrival and waited for the fateful day to finally come.

"One of us will accompany you as your lady in waiting," Crazy explained as we got the horses ready for the journey to the palace.

"I'll do it," Ugly volunteered much to my chagrin.   It was no secret that I got along much better with Crazy.   I wondered if Ugly wanted to come because she thought it would take too much of a toll on her older sister or if she just wanted to keep me in line.

"Are you sure you want to be at the palace when we most risk being discovered?" I asked with one eyebrow raised in disdain.

"There's no way we'll be found out with me present to make certain you don't mess up," she haughtily replied.

"Please attempt to get along," Crazy begged us.   "It will be detrimental to us all if our ruse is revealed."

"I'll try my best for your sake and mine," Ugly promised.   I rolled my eyes at the obvious omission.

Crazy helped me onto my bridled horse.   "Safe journey, your Majesty," she said with a dramatic curtsey.

"Thank you for everything," I replied.   "I'll send word as soon as I have secured my position as the King's fiancée."

I spent the ride into town visualizing success.   It wasn't always easy with Ugly's constant yawning and sighing in boredom.

"Could you please get into character?" I asked her.

"Quit worrying so much!" she said disgruntled.   "There's no one in sight.   I'll put on a performance that will blow you away when it matters." Now I was the one sighing.

Finally, we arrived at the edge of town and our charade began.   My posture was as prim and proper as I could muster.   I saw the villagers staring, but made eye contact with no one, as if I was above their lives of mediocrity.   We made our way to the castle gate and were halted.   I simply handed the guard the letter of invitation, complete with the King's seal, and we were allowed through the gateway and into the immense courtyard.

We were assisted off our horses, then the servants took our bags inside while the horses were lead to the stables.   We were ushered inside the palace foyer.   A woman guided us to a beautiful parlor and brought us tea and scones.   I was now so nervous to have made it this far that I stared at the china pattern on the cup from which I was sipping.   There were hand painted flowers edged in gold and a bumblebee so lifelike it nearly made me jump out of my chair.   I stayed distracted in my own thoughts until the servant announced, "I will inform the King that you have safely arrived."

"Might we be shown to our rooms and given a chance to refresh before being introduced to his Majesty?" I interjected.

"Of course you may," she said as if she were afraid she'd risked offending me.   "Please follow me."

She lead the way up the grand main staircase and to the wing where the guest rooms were located.   The room she took us to was familiar to me; it was where Princess Pearl resided prior to wedding the King.   Not a thing had changed in that room since I did her dress fittings all those years ago.   The windows were still covered by chardonnay colored drapes.   The bed was a wrought iron canopy, lined with goose feather pillows.   There was a bouquet of brilliant white lilies on a cedar chest at the foot of the bed. Everything looked cozy and bright.

There was a door adjoining to a smaller room meant for Ugly.   It was simple and neat containing a bed with white sheets, a small table and a chair.   A vase of daisies on the table and a crucifix on the wall were the only decorations.

"I'll leave you now, so you can rest.   You may join the King for dinner in the banquet hall at seven o'clock," the servant said before exiting.

After she left, Ugly let out a snort.   "I can't be expected to sleep in that room!" she said as she pointed to the annex.

"Why not?" I asked.   "The bedroom in your cottage is hardly any bigger, and it's clean and comfortable."

"Comfortable?!"   she said in disdain.   "Crosses make me uneasy," she said as she grabbed the crucifix off the wall.

"Could you please try to behave yourself?" I begged her.   Then I reminded her, "If they suspect that anything is amiss, it will be our downfall."

"Be that as it may, I am not sleeping in the same room as God," she declared as she shoved the cross in a dresser drawer in my own room.   I shook my head and envisioned a successful interlude with the King so I could send Ugly packing for home.

The servants must have brought our bags to my room while we were enjoying our tea.   I opened the satchels and pulled out three of the amazing gowns I had made.   As I hung them in the wardrobe, I wondered out loud, "Which one should I wear to dinner?"

"The scarlet one," was Ugly's assessment of the situation, though I wasn't really asking for her opinion.   "Nothing makes a man more passionate than when he's seeing red."

A buried memory began to surface like the unpleasantness of a knife being thrust into my thigh.   I needed to retain my composure and calm my breathing.   It was okay.   These memories were just reminders of why I was here right now.   I would soon have full control of my life once more.

While I was lost in thought, I was startled back to reality by a knock on the door.   I motioned to Ugly to play the servant role and answer the door. "Who goes there?" she asked in her most polite voice.

"It is his royal Majesty, here to welcome Princess Lilith to Whitebirchburg," another servant's voice replied.   My heart began to pound rapidly.   I didn't expect to meet the King until the banquet.   Ugly was already opening the door when I realized the improvisation started now.

"Your highness, it's such a pleasure to finally meet you in person," I announced in the sweetest tone I could manage.

"Princess, I hope you don't think it too forward of me to visit you before dinner, but I was just so anxious to see you at last!" he said with genuine enthusiasm. "Could you please excuse us," he said to the servants. Ugly left with the others, closing the door behind her as she went.

The King was tall with broad shoulders and a rugged physique. His hair was a dark ebony, but his eyes were a lighter hazel that offset his ruddy complexion. He wasn't bad looking, but he wasn't handsome either. I worried that the lack of spark between us would be too obvious, but apparently these feelings were merely one-sided. The King grabbed me in a large embrace and held me for several minutes. I found this behavior most presumptuous to someone he had just barely met.

"Princess Lilith, you are more beautiful than your portrait led me to believe," he said in ecstatic awe. "You are more fair than the day lilies in this arrangement," he said motioning to the flowers on the cedar chest.

"You flatter me, kind Sir," I said in reply.

"Nonsense! I only know how to speak the truth. Those flowers will wilt with envy before the day is through," he declared. "In fact, the only person I know with skin as porcelain fair as yours is my seven year old daughter, Snow White."

"Snow White, what a darling name!" I lied, as I thought the name quite atrocious - simple, silly and sugary sweet.

"Then you, my dear, I shall call Lily White, since it suits you so well!" he said with a chuckle, amused by his own cleverness.

I despised it at once, yet replied, "I've never been called something so endearing.   You really shouldn't make it a habit!"

"My mind is made up.   You are more delicate and sweet than any flower in this kingdom; no one is more deserving of the name Lily White." Thus, I was stuck with a name I found more revolting than Piggy.   I smiled with forced effort.   What on earth did Princess Pearl see in this man?

"You are too kind," I said as I attempted to guilt him on his unannounced intrusion.   "I'm terribly sorry that you are seeing me in my traveling ensemble.   I promise to make a better impression tonight at dinner."

"Darling, Lily White, I look forward to it.   Now let me depart so you may rest from your journey before the feast begins," he said much to my relief.   Before leaving, he leaned in and kissed my cheek.   Goosebumps formed on my arms from disgust rather than excitement.

I sat on the bed alone, contemplating the situation.   This was going to be more difficult than I anticipated.   How could I kiss a man and win his heart when he made me want to vomit?   I was lost in these thoughts when Ugly slipped back in and jumped on the bed by my side.   She wrapped her arms around me gleefully and said, "I just followed the King a short distance, and he seems quite smitten with you!   Tell me all the details, Piggy!"   Ugly was such a sight to behold - an old hag behaving like a giddy adolescent.   But it suddenly felt so good to be in her company and called Piggy once more.   Tears began to form in the corners of my eyes.   "Piggy, what's wrong?"

"I can't stand him!   I guess I never really thought this plan through.   I suppose I never really expected it to work or assumed I would like the King well enough to get by...but I truly hate him!"   I began to burst into sobs.

"Lower your voice," Ugly warned.   "You never know who could be spying on us." I tried to muffle my sorrow with a goose feather pillow. "What makes him so awful?"

"He's a syrupy sweet romantic who has given me the special honor of being called Lily White," I said as Ugly burst into a fit of giggles.   "It's not funny!   He kissed my cheek here, in this room that remains a shrine to his dead wife!   How cruel to insult the deceased in such a manner!"

"Don't be so melodramatic, Piggy!" advised Ugly.   "He sounds annoying, but lonely.   He already holds you in the same esteem as his late wife; our plan is working all too well!"

"But what good is being Queen, if I'm miserable?" I lamented.

"Patience, my dear," Ugly tried to soothe me in her own way.   "Life with the King need not be...permanent."

I suddenly stopped sobbing and looked at her face in disbelief.   She shook her head in an affirmative motion.   I'd never contemplated death as being part of the equation of me being Queen.   But as I looked at Ugly, I realized that Crazy and her had calculated this scenario long ago.   Was it wrong that I felt a sudden sense of relief?   Ugly saw the calmness that settled over me.

"Remember, Piggy, the King does not love you, but Lily White.   Who you really are   cannot be taken from you.   Lily is a means to an end.   I know you can portray her believably until you become the Queen."

"Yes, Ugly, I know that I can.   It's just…" but I could not bring myself to finish the thought.

"What?" Ugly insisted.

"I'm afraid I am losing who I truly am.   I never would've considered harming any living person before, let alone the King.   My moral compass tells me how wrong it is and yet…I somehow no longer care.   I guess I am a bad person at the core."   I hated to admit the fact.

Ugly just giggled again.   "You're not a nice person, that's for certain, but then again, who really is?   There's no fun in being nice."

I felt a war waging within myself.   Were my aspirations for the future worth destroying others' lives?   My head told me I was being selfish and wicked, but looking at Ugly's devious grin gave me the nerve to proceed.

"So, the red dress it is," I said as Lily White prepared to seduce the dimwitted King.

The feast in honor of my arrival was unlike anything I had ever experienced.   The guests all had their eyes on me, and there was so much to eat and drink that I couldn't help but try everything.   Ugly got so intoxicated that I finally decided that this was the true reason she chose to come with me.

When the meal concluded, we all headed out to the turret and watched fireworks being released into the night sky. If the King wanted a new wife, he was going all out to impress her. I thought it all rather desperate and pathetic, but Lily White quite approved, and the King could not have been happier.

"If you don't mind me inquiring," the King leaned over to ask, "why is your lady-in-waiting so old?"

"She was the nanny who raised me," I said as the lies came easily to me now. "She's the most trusted of my servants, which is why I wanted her to come."

"But don't you think it unkind to make an elderly woman make such a journey?" the King asked.

I glanced at Ugly in her flirty, drunken state and replied, "She seems no worse for wear."

"No, I suppose she doesn't," the King chuckled. "The air is growing bitter, would you like to return inside?"

"Is there somewhere we can be alone? There's something I'd like to confide in you privately," I said in a mysterious tone.

"Of course," he said too eagerly as he led me down a long hallway and into a sitting room. There was no one inside, and he locked the door behind him as we entered. "Make yourself comfortable and tell me what's on your mind."

"Well," I began hesitantly, "there has been internal conflict within my kingdom."

"Go on," the King urged. "I will help out however possible, so please hold nothing back."

"My father is quite ill and my younger brother is set to succeed him to the throne.   There should be no issue in regard to this matter, except that my brother distrusts me.   I have no interest in politics, myself, but he was given the bad advice to fear my position.   In our kingdom, a Princess can usurp her brother, if he is proven to be incompetent.   A rumor was spread that I intended to do just that, but in truth, I don't want the responsibility of the crown, nor do I think my brother unfit to rule.   Still, my brother has informed me that after our father's death, I would be banished.   I hope you don't think me too forward, but I came to you hoping you would grant me sanctuary.   I know it's unfair to involve you in our conflict, but I don't wish to return to my land and have everyone scowl at me, as if I were a woman of ill intent."   At this point, I began to sob as if the burden of losing my father and being abandoned by my brother was too much heartache for me to bear.

The King was an empathetic man, and he ate up the story Crazy prepared for me.   He put his arm around me so I could cry on his shoulder. "My dearest, you may stay here as long as you desire," he promised in a soothing tone.

"Even if it should be forever?" I pouted as I gazed into his tender eyes.

"I hope it will be," was his heartfelt reply.   Then he leaned over and kissed my mouth to seal the deal.   Though I was gagging on the inside, I closed my eyes to block out what was occurring and reminded myself that this moment was crucial and all would soon be mine.   I felt my face turn red in disgust at him, but myself as well.   He must have thought I was blushing from innocence.

"I don't mean to rush things, but I would be happy to make you my bride.   Let me take care of you, and you won't ever have to worry about your brother again."

"Are you asking me to marry you?" I asked in a voice full of delightful surprise.

"Lily White, would you do me the honor of becoming my wife?" he formally asked.

"I will!" I answered with true joy spilling from my lips, though for a reason much different than his.

The rest of the evening was a bit of a blur.   We hugged, danced, drank and shared stories.   At midnight, he finally accompanied me back to my room.   "We'll announce our engagement at breakfast," he said and kissed my forehead.

"Sleep well, darling," I said as I slipped into my room.   I saw the wilted petals scattered across the cedar chest, just as the King predicted.   I immediately jumped on the bed and started laughing.   Ugly crept out of her room, clearly feeling the effects of her alcohol consumption.

"Keep it down!   What's wrong with you?!" she shouted in her typical annoyed demeanor.

But I just stayed bouncing on the bed happily.   I looked at her and announced, "It's done!"

The magnitude of my words reached her, and she climbed on the bed to join me, saying, "Already?   Are you sure?"

"He fell for Crazy's story in an instant.   I'm being introduced as his fiancée   in the morning!"

"I told you!" Ugly declared, now eager to take all the credit.   "That's the power of wearing red!" she said as she pointed to my dress.

"That's the power of impermanence!" I declared.

"That's the power of making a wager!" she reminded me as we held each other in a sisterly embrace.

"That's the power of beauty!" I said as I finally admitted to myself that Crazy and Ugly had been right all along.

Human Behaviour

"There's definitely no logic to human behaviour but yet so irresistible."

-Bjork

In the morning, I met her for the very first time. The King's beloved daughter was not the precious, adorable child I was expecting, but rather an awkward and clumsy girl who had gaping holes in her mouth from recently losing her baby teeth. I may have disliked the King, but I instantly hated his offspring. I can't to this day pinpoint what about the child offended me so, but I just knew that I would never like her. Alas, she was a package deal with the King, and so I was forced to compromise my comfort level yet again. I decided early on that the best way to deal with Snow White would simply be to ignore her, as I didn't have it in me to dote on her as some substitute mother.

Again, I was reminded that the title of Queen came at an increasingly large price. I would also become wife and stepmother - two roles I absolutely despised. Strangely enough, even though Ugly's suggestion that the King need not live forever set my mind at ease, I never once thought of this as a possibility for his daughter. I guess I saw her merely as a child, not an actual person who would grow and age and one day be a woman. Nor could I imagine purposely killing a child.   Maybe I was a better person at the time than I am today.   Regardless, I saw Snow White's life linked to mine by a thin thread that could not be cut but might tear on its own if given enough wear.

Arrangements for the wedding were quickly underway.   I sent Ugly home to inform Crazy of my progress.   Soon a letter arrived from Lily White's brother informing her that her father was deceased and she was not allowed to enter the kingdom again, not even for the funeral.   This only encouraged the King to hurry our wedding celebration, rather than let his fiancée remain distressed by losing her family.

The day of the wedding dress fitting, my stomach churned with anticipation.   I fully expected my mother to still be the royal seamstress. I could barely sleep the night before as I envisioned the look of surprise on her face and how exactly I would explain myself to her.   Would she be proud?   Disappointed?   I really couldn't guess.   It was hard to know if she would admire my cleverness in marrying the King or if she'd be disgusted by the lies and deceit.   Certainly, she would approve of using a man rather than being used by one, but I somehow doubted she would think it worth the price of suppressing my inner self.

So, when I opened the door to my room and allowed the seamstress to come in, I was confused to see a woman nearly my own age standing before me.

"You seem surprised to see me, Princess.   You did know that you were being fit for your gown today, didn't you?" she asked me as she unfolded the massive white satin fabric.

"Yes, it's just that you seem so young.   Have you been royal seamstress for very long?" I asked as I dreaded her reply.

"Only about a year.   The previous seamstress went mad when her only daughter left her.   In a fit of hysteria, she poisoned herself!   Can you imagine?"

"What?!" I exclaimed in disbelief.   "Did she die?"

"Of course," the maiden replied in puzzlement.   "That is the result of suicide.   Still, her bad luck was my good luck, as you can clearly see."

And all at once, I snapped.   "Get out of here at once, you heartless wench!   I don't need you; I'll make the dress myself!   Get out!   GET OUT!"   The woman was so frightened by my screaming that she left her things and fled as quickly as she could.

The servants, no doubt, heard it all and were on their way to summon the King.   I cried hysterically, knowing the truth.   My mother had not died of suicide, but matricide.   It was I who broke her heart.

Suddenly, the King was at my side, trying his best to calm his frantic bride.   "Dearest, what's wrong?"

"The seamstress just insulted my family!" I declared.   "I fired her!"

"I understand," the King said.   "We'll send for someone new right away."

"No!" I shouted, knowing that I could not bear anyone else.   "I'll do it myself.   I know how to sew.   Please, let me just do it myself."

"Lily White, you don't need to bother yourself while you're still grieving for your father.   You're not being rational right now.   Let someone else take care of this for you," he attempted to reason with me.

"I said I'd do it!" I shrieked.

"Calm down, Lily.   You can do whatever makes you happy, but you need not decide on what that is this very moment."

"I need to be alone right now," I said as I looked at him through bleary eyes.

He kissed the top of my head and said with a sigh, "I wish I could take your pain away or suffer it in your place."   Then he left the room, and I examined the lace, beads, bows and satin and immediately went to work. I would create a gown that my mother would've been proud to see me wearing.   I worked like a mad woman just to prove to myself that I could do it.   The end result was magnificent, but I wondered if the kingdom would be able to tell that this dress was lined with tears of sadness rather than joy?

Perhaps I played the role of bereaved daughter more accurately now. I decided to consider it a parting gift from my mother, who I figured would indeed have approved of my deception here on Earth, but was watching me from the afterworld with unforgiveness for abandoning her.   Why would she forgive me?   I certainly didn't plan to forgive myself.   If I had returned to my mother and confessed to her the truth instead of living with Ugly and Crazy, she might still be alive today.   And with my mother alive, I might have found a way to be the content person I once was.   Instead, I strived to do things on my own terms and look where it led me?   Now I had no choice but to finish what I started.

The wedding day quickly arrived and passed by in a blur of activity.   I can recall bits and pieces of the day, as if reconstructing a dream that I can't quite remember.   I can see all the kingdom looking at me with envy, just as I looked at Princess Pearl years ago.   I know that Snow White's hair was done in ringlets that for once made her look more precious than precocious, and that she stood by her father's side during our vows.   I remember exchanging rings, but not the words of our vows, which is just as well since I had no intention of abiding by them.   I know that my wedding dress was a sight to behold with a train that cascaded down the aisle and made Pearl's dress look quite ordinary by comparison.   I remember that there was an abundance of champagne that made the day merry for all.   Even though I was playing pretend and didn't actually love the King, I did quite enjoy the wedding feast.   Why wouldn't I?   It was a celebration in my honor and truly tasted of victory.   I had achieved what I had set out to do and could not have felt happier in that moment.

Even when the day had ended and the time had arrived for us to consummate our union in the marriage bed, I was not nervous.   I felt triumphant.   The King turned out to be a satisfactory lover, which once again assured me that I could play my role well.

The days following the wedding truly felt like a honeymoon period.   I was doted on by the King and servants alike.   I was living in a palace, eating the finest foods and wearing the most exquisite gowns.   Everyone hung on my every word.   All my needs and requests were promptly answered.   I was surrounded by books, gardens, sunshine and adoration. Once again, I felt in control of my life, and for the first time in a very long time, I was happy.

Then the day came when it arrived. A huge crate was delivered by a man with a cart who proclaimed that it was a wedding gift to the Princess from her beloved brother. I knew this meant it was actually from Crazy and Ugly, so I eagerly waited for the servants to pry open the package and reveal the gift. When they removed it from the crate, I saw that it was flat and long and covered with the quilt I had slept with for the past year. When the quilt was taken off, there stood a beautiful, gilded mirror. I wondered where the sisters had obtained it. I told the servants to hang it in my dressing room as I folded up the quilt and tried to decided if I wanted to keep or dispose of this remnant of my recent past.

Just then, Snow White came skipping up to me and said, "Stepmother, I'm about to have a tea party with my dollies. Would you like to join us?"

"No, I'm busy right now, but here," I said as I handed her the quilt. "You may have this for your tablecloth."

"Thank you, stepmother," she said enthusiastically as she hurried back to her room.

Then I headed to my study and enjoyed a cup of tea by myself. I got lost in a good book until a servant fetched me for dinner. Once I ate my fill on another gourmet meal I headed to my quarters to enjoy a warm bath.

I had forgotten all about the sisters' present until I got to my dressing room and was startled by my own reflection. I approached the mirror wondering if they had sealed it with magick.   Maybe it was a portal back to their home or a way to communicate my thoughts to them and theirs to me. I ran my fingers over the ornate perimeter, but nothing happened as I was left staring at my own reflection.   I could scarcely believe how beautiful I was and then I realized why they had sent me the mirror.   It wasn't made of any kind of magick; it was merely a reminder of our wager.   They would make me beautiful and grant me the power to gain control by marrying the King, and I would help them gain eternal youth.   This was to let me know that they were holding me accountable to my promise.   I glanced once more at the mirror in disgust, disrobed and soaked in my claw foot bathtub as I considered what I had to do.

Suddenly, I was overwhelmed by an undeniable wave of guilt.   Since the wedding, I'd been smiling and enjoying my life, despite the fact that I was responsible for killing my mother.   Crazy and Ugly were waiting for me to repay their favor while I secretly hoped to never see them again.   I even shunned Snow White for no reason at all.   I really wasn't a good person, but worse still, I didn't want to be!   The guilt was eating me up, and the longer I remained in the tub trying to get clean, the dirtier I felt.

Finally, I emerged from the tub, my skin wrinkled from lingering in the water too long.   I returned to my new dressing mirror and stood before it naked, assessing my imperfections.   My hair was tousled and dripping wet, my eyes were puffy from shedding frustrated tears and my belly had grown round from indulging in so much fine cuisine.   I closed my eyes and said out loud, "Looking glass, upon the wall, who is fairest of us all?"

When I opened my eyes, I saw my reflection staring back.   Despite the flaws, I was, in fact, still beautiful.   I must have seemed mad, but I began to howl in laughter.   Yes, of course, being beautiful had taken me this far, but I was not yet beautiful enough.   I needed beauty that would absolve me of my guilt; beauty that would transform my soul as well as my body.

I put on my robe and ran into my study.   I lit a candle on my desk and sat down and wrote the following letter to Crazy and Ugly.

Your gift arrived safely intact, and I thank you for your generosity. It will remind me daily of our agreement.   With your help, I have come this far, but the remaining journey is my own.   I will continue to believe in the power of beauty, but am not yet convinced of your position.   After all, I have not yet been made Queen.   Therefore, there is something specific that I must do before I will be able to return the favor to you.   Fear not, I am a woman of my word, and I intend to help you both, after I have helped myself.   Patience and good health be with you in the meantime.

Warm regards,   Piggy

Raise It Up

"I must become the lion hearted girl, ready for a fight, before I make the final sacrifice." – Florence Welch

I wanted the King to give me a baby. It wasn't because I was trying to strengthen my claim to the throne or even diminish that of Snow White, but my reasons were purely selfish nonetheless. I thought the pain of losing my mother might lessen if I were to become a mother myself. I didn't care if I had a boy or a girl, I just knew that I wanted to be pregnant immediately.

Obviously, the King was not opposed to my voracious sexual appetite. But as the months passed by and still I bled, my frustration turned into anger against the King. The only time I wanted him near me was to share my bed. I came up with all manner of excuses to ignore him throughout the day.

I was in complete denial that the problem conceiving might be mine. Fed up with the King, I amassed a following of lovers on the side. I figured that if I become impregnated by someone else, the King would never know the difference. The silence of these other men was bought by my power. If an adulterous affair should be revealed, their lives were the ones in jeopardy.

Again the months passed by to no avail.   Then the realization was too evident to ignore - I could not bear a child.   The King had a baby with Princess Pearl during their first year of union.   The problem at hand was clearly mine, not his.

I sunk into a deep depression and found myself crying all the time. Once again, the thing I most wanted was not within my control.   I was a woman obsessed.   I hated all the pregnant women I saw.   I hated all the mothers I saw with newborn babies.   This was a new form of envy.   It was a jealousy that enraged me because I could not change my situation despite my unrelenting attempts.   When I heard folks complain about the discomfort of pregnancy or whine about their baby crying all night, I would fume at their ungratefulness, knowing that they took for granted the most precious gift in the world!

My life became a cycle of anger and sadness.   I would cry myself to sleep and then wake up and cry some more.   I wept so much that I was surprised that I didn't ever run out of tears.   I was constantly excusing myself so I could sob or scream, depending on the situation, without completely humiliating myself.

On our first wedding anniversary, the King decided he needed answers as to why his bride was so temperamental.   As we sat in our bedchamber eating cake to celebrate the occasion, he looked at me and said, "Lily White, I love you madly, but you seem much sadder than you were a year ago. Won't you tell me what's wrong, so I can help you?"

"There's nothing you can do to help," I said matter-of-factly.   "It's a problem that simply cannot be fixed."

"Even so, talking about it might help," he urged. "I am always here to listen."

I sighed and decided to confess. "I want to have a baby, but don't believe that I can." The shame of those words nearly killed me to speak them out loud.

"Is that all?" he laughed. "To be honest, I'm much relieved to discover you cannot. I lost my first wife in childbirth and am quite terrified to repeat it! I gained a daughter, but lost a wife. Now that I have a wife again, I aim to keep her. Fear not, Lily, I don't desire any more children," the King assured me.

What an arrogant man! He failed to realize that this wasn't about what he wanted, but what I wanted! His relief became my new frustration. Still, I played the part of Lily White, the King's obedient and submissive wife. I dabbed my eyes with a napkin and forced myself to smile.

"Blessings come in an assortment of ways," the King continued. "Sometimes not having a child is as much a gift as having one. In the end, we still have each other."

"I'm stuck with you alright!" I said as I raised another forkful of cake to my lips.

The King missed the sarcasm and chuckled again. "And we still have Snow White to dote upon," he added.

"We sure do," I said through an insincere grin.

An undeniable sense of failure penetrated me to the depths of my soul as the years began to pass. Strangely enough, even though my experiences seemed to disprove Crazy and Ugly's position that beauty would grant me control, I became more and more obsessed with my personal appearance. It was like hiding behind a mask in order to conceal the truth. The more beautiful I became, the less it appeared that anything could be wrong with me.

I kept out of the sun to maintain my fair complexion and never allowed anyone to see me unless my face was painted on, including the King. I ate smaller portions during meals in order to get a flat belly. Everyday I tried my best to make the laces on my corset tighter than the previous day. The reason was that I didn't want anyone to mistake me for being pregnant. If wide hips and a swollen belly were fashionable because they represented fertility, then I would start my own trend. Brushing and fixing my hair was also a daily ritual that I sometimes devoted more than an hour doing. It all became a game to me after awhile. How small could my waist be? How long could my hair grow? I would gain control of the things that I could control, and I would do it the way I knew how - by being beautiful.

At this point, I was so immersed in my beauty regime that I never pondered whether it was rational or not. My behavior had become automatic. For the most part, it gave me something to focus on and kept me distracted from the reasons that prompted this response. Still there were days when the pretty exterior could not keep me from feeling miserable within. On those occasions, I would worry that everyone could look right through me and sense my heartache and shame, but no one ever indicated to me that they did.

All the while, Snow White grew to be more of a nuisance every day. This was not the child that I longed to hold in my arms. She was spoiled and noisy, and I could not avoid her enough.

My life began to settle into a routine. Everyday was the same. I buried my feelings of guilt, rage and misery under a layer of silk gowns, rouge and hairpins. I successfully concealed the real me from those around me and sometimes even from myself.

One morning began like any other - the King attended to his duties, Snow White was sent her morning porridge, and I was in my sitting room enjoying some tea. Then a servant emerged, carrying a letter. "Forgive the intrusion, your highness, but there are two women at the front gate requesting an audience with you. They didn't leave their names, but claim you will know their identities by this." He handed me an envelope that was sealed with black wax and stamped with a bird. I knew immediately who it was from, but pretended for the sake of my servant that I did not and pulled out the enclosed letter and read:

To our beloved Lilith,

   The time has come for you to keep old promises. In return, we shall help you yet again. Long live the Queen!

Affectionately yours,

Charlotte and Ursula

"You may let them in," I told the servant and then headed to my dressing room.   I wanted to wear something regal, so I put on an embroidered red and black gown with a matching velvet cloak.   I affixed a gold tiara embedded with rubies to my hair and checked my appearance in the ornate mirror.   I told myself that I would not be intimidated.   I announced to my reflection in the looking glass, "Now you witches will see who is fairest of all!"

I made my way down the grand main staircase to the castle foyer. The King was there to greet me at the bottom.

"Dearest, I'm told that we have unexpected guests?" he said, clearly concerned for my safety.

"Yes, darling, let me introduce you to my great aunts, Ursula and Charlotte," I answered as I hugged the two elderly women who stood before me.   They had aged so rapidly since I last saw them that I knew the King would never recognize Ugly from having met her previously.

"Welcome!" the King gladly proclaimed.   "My wife so rarely has visitors, please stay with us as long you desire."

"Oh, yes, we certainly will," Ugly replied.   I realized quickly that her attitude was quite unchanged.

"Now if you'll excuse me, I have business to attend to, so I'll leave you ladies to become reacquainted."   The King left, and I turned to the witches and wondered how I could get them to leave the most quickly.

"Dear aunts, it's been too long.   Please follow me to my private wing and we shall have some tea," I said as I lead the way.

"Travel has worn us out.   I trust you can give us something to eat as well?" Ugly inquired.

"Of course," I answered.

We sat down in my sitting room, and I had the kitchen staff bring us an array of brunch items: poached eggs, sweet rolls, slices of honey glazed ham, and fresh fruit.   Ugly began to eat as if she'd been starving for days, but Crazy nibbled with little interest, as if she had no appetite.

"It's been five years," Crazy began.

"Has it?"   I asked.   We sat in silence for several minutes.

Crazy tried to begin the conversation again.   "As you can plainly see, we haven't gotten any younger."

"Run out of boar hearts, have you?" I asked, bemused by their own misfortune.

"Oh, Piggy, you're still so funny!" Ugly sarcastically declared.

"Are we dropping formalities, Auntie Ursula?"   I asked.

"Not in front of your darling husband, of course," Ugly maintained.

"But for now, we can cease the pretense," Crazy added.   "Let's get straight to the point.   You know why we're here."

"I imagine you have a plan in mind?" I inquired, as I knew Crazy did everything deliberately with a specific goal.

"Obviously, we came prepared," Crazy informed me.

"Well, that's a relief," I said.   "I don't make it a habit to keep jars of animal entrails laying around like you ladies.”

"Sheesh," Ugly grunted.   "What kind of witch have you become?”

"You can cut out the adorable sarcasm, Piggy," Crazy said, clearly not amused.   "Your role will be rather minimal, so you need not complain. Especially given all we have done for you.”

I sneered at the sisters.   "You give yourselves too much credit.   You helped me wed the King.   I am beautiful, but I am not happy and I do not have the control you promised me.”

"That is your own fault," Crazy declared.   "You create your own happiness - no one can do it for you!”

"I owe you nothing!" I maintained.

"You owe us everything!" Ugly screamed back as she slammed her fist on the table.   We sat quietly for several minutes, trading frosty glares with each other.

"We gave you more than an adequate timeframe to offer your assistance on a voluntary basis.   Now we do things our way," Crazy insisted.

"What is it you need me to do?" I relented in asking.

"You need to find us two suitable maidens that we can sacrifice," Ugly blurted out.

"Our elderly bodies make this a difficult task for us, but your position of power makes it an easy chore for you," Crazy added.

"Well, aren't you in luck!" I exclaimed.   "We're holding public executions in the town square this afternoon.”

"Perfect," Crazy said, though knowing her, she was already aware of this detail,   hence why they chose today to arrive.   "We'll need you to inspect the prisoners in advance and find the two that best meet our requirements."

"They must be young, as lovely as possible and virgins," Ugly emphasized, as though I'd forgotten.

"And what am I to do?   Feed the criminals boar meat as their last meal?"

"That's not necessary," assured Crazy.

"We only need the boar heart to act as a conduit if we're drinking blood.   These girls are going to die anyway, therefore we can eat their hearts directly and take advantage of the full impact of the spell," Ugly explained.   My face grew pale at the thought.   Ugly smirked.   "That's right, Piggy.   We went easy on you on our first encounter."

"You also neglected to verify my qualifications," I reminded her.

"We should've guessed you were actually a slut," Ugly said with a sigh.

I slammed a plate on the edge of the table and held a pointed shard to her throat.   "Listen up and listen good, you ugly witch!   Insult me again and you'll get no help from me today or evermore!"

"Must you two always be so dramatic?" Crazy sputtered.   "We'll leave you, Piggy, so you can get to work and we can get some rest."

I dropped the broken piece and headed for the door.   "You may finish your meal, and I will send a servant by shortly to show you to your room. I'll inform you when the deed is done."   With a swirl of my cape, I left the sisters behind and headed towards the gallows.

Disturbia

"It can creep up inside you and consume you, a disease of the mind,

It can control you, I feel like a monster."   – Rihanna

I put on my fur trimmed boots and a heavier cloak, as there was a chill in the air and headed outdoors.   Snow White was in the courtyard skipping rope.

"Stepmother, where are you going?   May I come with you?" she innocently inquired.

"I am headed into town, and no, you may not," I said in a huff.

"Why not?" she stomped her foot in opposition.

"Because it pertains to adult business," I snapped.

"I wish you'd stop treating me like a child!" she exclaimed.

"Then stop behaving like one!" I said as I left her behind.   I thought I glanced her sticking her tongue out at me as I left, but it may have been my imagination.   Either way, I certainly didn't have time for her foolishness today.   I hurried on my way, assured the guards at the palace gate that I didn't require an escort to the village and continued towards the town square.

My stomach churned as I glanced at the row of nooses hanging.   I counted a total of twenty.   I made my way to the executioner.   "Escort me to the condemned," I demanded.

"They are being read their final rites, your highness," he explained.

"I won't interfere with the clergy," I promised.   "I just wish to see their faces."

"Not all of them are repentant," he warned me.

"I understand," I replied.

He lead the way to a holding bin.   The prisoners were shackled together and standing in a line.   Some were on their knees with hands folded in prayer as the priest recited the twenty-third psalm.   Some others grunted, and a few had tears in their eyes.   Most looked scared with anticipation; some looked relieved, as if they'd already accepted their fate. Of the twenty, fifteen were men.   One of those was a child, no more than ten.   I didn't dare ask what his crime was.

Of the five women, only two looked to be a suitable age.   I looked into their eyes and saw no fear despite their circumstances.   I couldn't comprehend it.   If I had no control over my future, I would be going mad! The priest walked over to the girls with a bucket of water and said, "Daughters of God, I fear for your eternal souls and insist that you be baptized in the Lord's name before it is too late."   One of the girls spat on the priest while the other one cackled in laughter.   The priest, in his anger, threw the water on the maidens and said, "May God have mercy on your souls!"   He gathered up his rosary beads and bible and stormed off, humiliated.   Even though they were soaked to the bone on an already chilly day, the girls looked at each other and began to laugh again.   Their fearlessness gave them a beauty that frightened me.

"I need to talk to those women," I told the executioner.   "What crime are they charged with?"   I feared he would say prostitution.

"They were caught practicing witchcraft," he said in disgust.   His answer made me feel dizzy.   I looked again at these young women, who were perhaps no different from myself.   I left the executioner's side and slowly approached the prisoners.

"Speak your names," I demanded of the dripping wet girls.

"Ruby and Willow are our Goddess names," the one with honey blonde hair revealed.   "I'm Ruby," she specified.

"We knew you would come," Willow said as she twirled her dark brown hair.

"How?" I asked, taken aback.

"We saw a vision in smoke appear to us over a ritual fire.   We burned sage in praise of your name," she continued.

"What is my Goddess given name?" I asked, not quite believing her.

"Pigtails," she replied.   Her answer was close enough to surprise me. I decided to use their confidence in me to my own advantage.

"The Goddess spoke to me as well," I informed them.   "She wanted me to ask if you have remained chaste?"

"Of course!" Ruby replied.

"We would never taint our bodies with the flesh of men," Willow said in disgust.

"Then I am to use my power of authority to grant you both a pardon," I assured them.   I took the crimson sash from my dress off my waist and tore it in half.   Then I tied one half around Ruby's left arm and the other around Willow's.   "I'll inform the executioner what these ribbons signify," I promised the young witches.

"Thank you, sister!" Ruby exclaimed.   "You have saved us from certain death, and we are indebted to you!"

The girls cried tears of relief and joy as I left their sides.   I returned to the executioner and asked, "Will the bodies be buried in a mass grave?"

"Yes, your highness."

"The two girls that I have marked with red ribbons should not be buried with the others.   They have been marked by the devil.   I want their hearts cut out and brought to me at the palace to dispose of personally. Then their bodies are to be burned on a pyre."

"It shall be done," the executioner assured me.

"Then I shall take my leave," I said.   I turned my back on the prisoners and began walking away.

After going a short distance, I heard the drums indicate that the condemned were now being moved into position.   A crowd was now gathered in the square to witness the proceedings.   At this point, Ruby and Willow were sure to know that I had betrayed them.   I had no desire to watch what was going to happen.   My feet doubled their pace, but I was halted in my tracks when I heard a female voice cry out, "What hypocrites to murder us, when your very own Princess Lilith is also a witch!"   I turned

174

and watched the gallows as the accused were hanged.   Everything appeared before my eyes in black and white, except for the red cloth around the girls' naked arms, blowing in the bitter breeze.   The mark on my thigh throbbed in pain.   Had I made the wrong choice?

Then I glanced at the final smirk on the young maidens' faces and realized how proud they were to attempt to destroy my reputation as they departed this world.   I continued on towards the palace, satisfied that they were dead, and I was very much alive.   I heard voices in the crowd shouting, "Blasphemy!"   "Long live Princess Lilith!"   I knew I still had the people's support, but did worry that Ruby and Willow had successfully planted a seed of doubt in their minds.

I returned to the castle and requested that a bottle of wine be brought to my room.   I planned to inebriate myself before having to deal with Crazy and Ugly.   However, as I was walking through the corridor, I spotted them in one of the parlors, along with Snow White.

"What do you think you're doing?" I demanded as I burst into the room.

"Your great aunties were playing a game with me, stepmother," Snow White revealed in an excited voice.   I glanced down at the table they were gathered around and saw an array of large, brightly painted cards scattered. I guessed that Crazy had made the cards herself, probably a long time ago. "They're predicting my future by using this special deck of cards," Snow White explained.

"How could you?" I asked the sisters in horror.   "If the King finds out..."

"We're merely playing a game," Ugly maintained.   "It's harmless fun."

"I won't tell Papa," Snow White promised, clearly worried that she had done something wrong.

"We could read your fortune next, if you'd like," Crazy offered.

"Absolutely not!"

"Stepmother, it really is fun!" Snow White defended the sisters. "Auntie Ursula told me that I'd fall in love with a Prince!"

"Of course you will - you're a Princess!   Who else would you marry, but a Prince?" I clarified for her.

"And Auntie Charlotte said that this card will determine my fate," she said as she held up a card with a women seductively biting into an apple. It resembled Eve in the garden of Eden, though I wasn't sure why a biblical image would appear on a witch's deck.   Nor did I know what the image foretold.

"That's enough, Snow White!" I said as I snatched the card from her small hands.   "Now run along!   I need to speak to my great aunts privately.   Tell your father that we will be unable to join you both for dinner."   She groaned with reluctance as I shooed her away.

"Have you both completely lost your minds?" I inquired.   "Exposing Snow White to your activities shows a severe lack of intelligence!"

"Relax!" Ugly insisted.   "You've become too wrapped up in the role you're playing here at the palace.   You've forgotten how to have a good time!"

"You have some nerve, not allowing us to attend dinner tonight," Crazy sulked. "We don't enjoy being treated like your dirty little secret."

"Don't worry," I assured her. "Your dinner is already on its way." As if on cue, a servant arrived at that very moment carrying a wooden box shaped like a heart.

"Your highness, the items you requested have arrived. Shall I leave it in your bedchamber while you visit with company?" he asked.

"No, you may leave it here on the table," I said. I was glad to see that the cards were quickly picked up as he made his entrance. "We don't wish to be disturbed the rest of the evening, no matter the reason. Please pass that message along."

"As you wish." I locked the parlor door after he left.

The irony of the box shape and its contents was not lost on me. But then again, anything it could have been delivered in - a silver platter, perhaps - would've been equally tacky.

I lit some candles and arranged them in a circle on the table, surrounding the box. "Shall we begin?" I asked the sisters. Crazy nodded affirmatively and Ugly's eyes danced with anticipation. I opened the box and the two bloody organs inside were shaped nothing like the box that held them. The stench was overwhelming as the odor of death permeated the room. I wanted to vomit and was instantly glad that I would not be partaking in the ritual.

Together they recited the following incantation:

"We sacrificed two maidens chaste,

So we could gain a younger face.

Beauty will mask our hidden truth,

And serve as our fountain of youth.

We drink this blood and eat this meat,

So that our spell will be complete."

The witches each grabbed a heart and began to choke them down. Just watching them gnaw at the raw meat made my skin crawl in repulsion. Never in my life did I think I would condone cannibalism, let alone be the one responsible for it.

I began to feel so ill that I turned my back on the sisters and stared out the window instead. In the distance, I could see smoke billowing from the pyre. It was hard to believe that Ruby and Willow were living and breathing just a few hours ago, and now their flesh was burning while their hearts were being devoured. The guilt of my decision overcame me at once, and I though I might faint.

I went over to the chaise and laid down with my eyes closed, trying to block out the gross images of my day. The psychological damage was inflicting real physical pain upon my body. My stomach churned, and the mark on my thigh burned as if it had been set on fire. The throbbing in my leg grew in intensity until I could no longer ignore it. I opened my eyes and was shocked to see a trail of blood dripping down my leg. Adrenaline rushed through my body, causing me to scream in panic.

Crazy and Ugly rushed to my side, trying to get me to keep quiet so I wouldn't alert the staff to anything amiss. They no longer appeared as old

hags, but as lovely women, younger than myself.   Although I had seen
them young before, this time their skin looked more radiant, their hair
vibrant and full, their eyes sparkled and they seemed surprisingly strong for
bodies so slim.   I had missed the actual transformation.   But no matter, I
knew it was them.

"Piggy, are you crazy?" Ugly whispered to me in a scolding voice.
"You mustn't draw attention to us!"   Crazy clasped her hand over my
mouth to prevent me from further screeching.   I pointed to the blood
spilling down my leg.   The two sisters gasped as Ugly lifted my skirt and
saw that the pentagram had burned deep into my flesh, scarring and
wounding me.   "Your witch's mark is signaling your betrayal," Ugly
stammered.   "You tricked us!"

"No!   Never!" I defended myself.   "Go look in the mirror - you are
young and beautiful!"   The sisters both released me so they could run over
to the mirror hanging on the wall and verify the truth.   They stayed there
several minutes, as if approving of every last freckle on their faces.   Their
vanity was fascinating to watch.   Although they seemed to have forgotten
about me, I finally admitted, "It wasn't you I betrayed today; it was two
other witches."

"What witches?" Crazy asked with sudden interest.

"Ruby and Willow," I spoke, "the two witches whose hearts you just
ate."

"We just ate what?!" Crazy said in disbelief.

"You fed us the flesh of sister witches?!" Ugly exclaimed in abhorrence.

179

"They were the only prisoners who met your stupid qualifications," I replied. "What choice did I have?"

"Um, you could've waited!" Ugly insisted.

"Really? Could I have? I'm pretty sure you were particularly impatient. Coming back empty handed didn't appear to be an option," I reminded her.

Ugly looked at me like she might rip my head off with nothing more than her fingernails. "You cursed us! You deceived us into eating their flesh so that they could haunt us forever!"

"What are you talking about? I did no such thing! They were going to die anyway!"

"A piece of their souls has now entered our bodies," Crazy tried to explain. "If it were an ordinary mortal heart, we would be able to control it. But a witch can use magick, so there will now be an internal struggle to gain control of our bodies."

"An internal battle of the witches?" I pondered. I began to snicker at the thought. "Maybe your personality could stand the improvement," I said to Ugly.

"I'll kill you!" Ugly shouted. "Having your mind overtaken and your being destroyed from the inside out is no laughing matter!"

"Why are you so worried? They were young and inexperienced; how could they overpower your minds?" I wondered.

"We allowed them to transform our bodies; we already granted permission for them to access our beings," informed Crazy.

"So...your pursuit of beauty may in fact be your downfall yet," I mused.

"Don't worry about us, Piggy...we won't give up without a fight," Ugly promised me.

"No, of course not," I said. "Come ladies, I have faith in you both." In truth, I was rooting for Willow and Ruby, but I was willing to say anything as long as Ugly and Crazy would finally leave me in peace. I ran over to a cabinet and pulled out two servant uniforms. "If you put on these clothes, you'll be able to move freely throughout the castle in disguise. You may stay tonight and safely take your leave in the morning. My debt to you is now paid, and I bid you farewell." I opened the parlor door and motioned for them to leave first. "Age before beauty," I insisted.

Given the circumstances, I was worried the sisters might do me bodily harm. After parting our separate ways, I wanted to run to the King and have him wrap his arms around me and protect me. But my leg was still aching, and I didn't want him to touch it. So, I disappeared to my own room and bolted the door. I washed the now dried blood on my leg and put on my nightgown. I stared at my reflection in the mirror. This day did not begin or end the way I had anticipated, but I was still beautiful and my mind still belonged to me.

For a moment I wondered what it would be like to have someone else's life experiences seep into my body. Someone else's past might see the world in a more optimistic light than I did. But my body would fail that person, and she would be as unable to be a mother as I was. Then despite our varying pasts, our futures would merge and be the same. Regardless

181

of whose mind my body hosted, the sense of failure would remain.   I'm not
sure why, but this thought comforted me and made me feel less alone than
I'd felt in a very long time.

Tragic Kingdom

"They're unaware what's behind castle walls,

But now it's written in stone, the King has been overthrown."

- Gwen Stefani

When I awoke in the morning, my leg was no longer sore. I checked Crazy and Ugly's room to be sure they had departed. Relieved that they were gone, I made a promise with myself to abandon witchcraft. It served its purpose, but my life was now stable, and I didn't wish to have it disrupted with so much drama again. I headed to the banquet hall to enjoy breakfast with the King and explain that my great aunts had to leave suddenly.

I sat down, surprised that the King was not yet there. As the servant brought me some tea, I asked her, "Where is my husband this fine morning?"

Her face grew pale, and she said, "Have you not heard, your Highness? His Majesty became violently ill last night; he's still in bed."

I dropped my teacup, and it clattered on the table, but did not break. "What?! Why was I not informed at once?"

"You asked not to be disturbed and had locked the door to the parlor," she reminded me.

Without waiting for any further explanation, I raced to the master bedroom. The King did not look well at all. His body was convulsing, he was vomiting blood and gasping for breath. I knew at once that this was no ordinary illness. I also knew who exactly was responsible. I ordered the servants to keep Snow White away, in case whatever spell was placed on the King was contagious. I'm not sure why I was being protective of the Princess; I guess I just didn't want Crazy and Ugly to wreak more havoc on Whitebirchburg than they already had.

I threw my arms around the King in an affectionate gesture. I never loved him, but I no longer hated him. He'd been my companion these past five years, and I didn't want to lose him like this.

I wondered when Crazy and Ugly had contact with the King - before I returned from the village or after their transformation? Did they poison him? Did they cast a spell upon him? Either way, I didn't have the antidote or know the reversal to use. I wasn't the experienced witch that they were; I felt completely hopeless to do anything but watch him die.

The royal physician, obviously, couldn't determine the cause of the King's illness. I, alone, knew that he was not going to recover and was inconsolable. Even the King, himself, tried to comfort me and assured me that he'd be fine. Whatever means the sisters used to take the King's life, it was slow and painful. Exactly one week after the witches had left, the King perished.

His passing left me incredibly guilt ridden. I knew that if we had never met, he would not have had such an untimely demise.   I missed all the small things he did for me - surprising me with gifts of jewelry, rubbing my feet if I was in a bad mood and tucking me into bed at night.   I felt equally guilty for all the things about him that I didn't miss - his overly romanticized vision of the world, the careless choices he made in ruling the kingdom and his dense stupidity for not seeing right through me as he should have all along.

My world became a whirlwind from that day forward.   Funeral arrangements were quickly underway.   Without a ruler, the people were eager to make me Queen.   Still, rumors were spilling from the lips of some that I was a witch responsible for murdering the King.   My coronation was pushed ahead of schedule before such doubt could spread like an infection within the kingdom.   When the crown was placed upon my head and the scepter handed to me, I trembled with sublime satisfaction.

My days were soon busy with official business.   There were so many decisions to be made each day.   It felt so good to be useful instead of dangling like a pretty ornament on the arm of the King.   For the first time ever, my life served a distinct purpose.

Without the King, I felt that no one was judging me on why I wasn't pregnant.   The expectation was gone, which felt like a huge weight had been lifted from my shoulders.   The sense of obsession and failure significantly diminished.

More than that, I finally had people's sympathy.   I was seen as the tragic widow.   My subjects respected my ability to carry on and be strong through such adversity.   I was a survivor, but had never been shown pity in times of hardship prior to this.   I had no idea how much I craved empathy until I had at last received it.

As Queen, my true self was able to thrive.   I was strict and effective in my command of the kingdom.   Farming and trading were both commodities that I oversaw and had running more efficiently than the King ever did.   Making the kingdom more profitable was proof of my success. Even if there were those who opposed my sharp tongue and no nonsense approach, they could not deny that my leadership got results.

I enjoyed being a busy woman in control of my domain.   The adage about time passing rapidly when you are happy seemed to hold true. Before I knew it, five years had passed.

One morning, I looked at my reflection in my dressing room mirror and saw a single strand of gray hair on my head.   I was in disbelief as I plucked it out.   A week later, I noticed several more.   A more intense scrutiny showed wrinkles forming beneath my eyes.   Age spots were appearing on my hands and arms as well.   I was still young, so why was I starting to look so old?

I cursed the stress of my position.   I had the control I had always dreamed of, but it was rapidly robbing me of my youth in the process.   I got dressed and tried my best to mask these increasing imperfections.

My bad mood was intensified when I was reminded that my agenda for the day consisted of smoothing out relations with a neighboring kingdom. Apparently, ties between our nations had deteriorated due to the actions of

the late King.   I resented cleaning up his messes, even after all these years.
Plus, I hated playing diplomat and having to act interested in matters that
bored me to tears.

On my way to the throne room, I heard the melancholy voice of a girl
singing to herself.   "An apple a day, will keep me away.   That's what they
say, so here I will play."   Though the voice was sad, it was still lovely.   I
peered into the room and saw Snow White arranging apple seeds into a
floral pattern on a table.

"Snow White, what are you doing?" I questioned the young woman.

"Good morning, stepmother," she said politely.   "The chef was coring
apples for making tarts, and I asked if I could have the seeds."

"Whatever for?"

"I don't know.   I just thought it would be fun to arrange a design with
them," she shrugged.

"It's a pointless activity.   If you can't find something useful to do with
your time, I'll decide for you," I threatened her.

She got up from the table and mumbled, "Don't worry about me.
There's plenty I can do today to stay out of your way."   She left the room
humming her tune while the apple seeds remained spread on the table.   I
shook my head at such nonsense and continued towards my destination.

I arrived at the throne room still thinking about my foolish
stepdaughter.   For such a clumsy child, she had blossomed into a very
pretty young woman.   Though she didn't paint her face on as I did, her fair
skin had a luminous glow that was such a contrast to her ebony hair and red

lips.   She'd lived through the hardships of losing both parents, but she exuded a naiveté about the world around her.   This innocence clung to her like perfume permeating from a rose.   This was her weakness, and I knew someday, I would use it against her.

Though I wasn't the one who poisoned Snow White's father, I now considered it to be the best thing that had ever happened to my life. Everyday, Snow White's beauty grew even as my own diminished. Therefore, she would need to be removed from my sight quite soon, lest I be driven mad with envy once again.   I just had to figure out how.

I'd barely been paying attention to my royal duties, when an announcement was made that our guests from the neighboring kingdom of Starlightdorf had arrived.   The King had sent his only son to personally handle the border dispute.   I knew this would be a simple matter requiring little fanfare.   Yet, as I was being introduced to the Prince, my mind started to scheme up a plan.   There was a perfect way for me to take care of two birds with one stone.   If I married Snow White off to this other kingdom, it would reconcile peace between our nations and get her out of my way for good!

I told the Prince we would have a banquet in his honor that evening.   I was certain that Snow White's beauty would be enough to charm him.   We adjourned our meeting, and I returned to my bedchamber delighted by my own brilliance.   Young girls were easily won over by a handsome face.   I would make Snow White's dream come true before she had time to process what was happening.   Getting rid of Snow White would be a much less messy matter than disposing of her father had been. "Thank you, Crazy and Ugly," I mused to myself, "but I've got this one!"

Before our guest arrived for dinner, I told Snow White that she was to be the Prince's bride. She shocked me when she began to vehemently protest. Was this the same girl who had been singing gloomily to apple seeds mere hours earlier? I was sure the Princess disliked me as much as I did her, so why was she not jumping at this opportunity?

Then the Prince appeared and things became even more interesting. Apparently, the two had already met. Snow White maintained her disinterest in the Prince, but he seemed outright confused by her aloofness. The Princess was playing some sort of game, but I couldn't determine if it was with me or the Prince.

Did she not want to appear too eager to run off with the Prince or did she truly dislike him? I found their entire exchange downright amusing. I really didn't care what happened to Snow White when she left here, but if she was not going to live happily ever after, I would consider it an added bonus. I ate my dinner while watching the drama unfold before my eyes. I hadn't been so entertained since the final departure of Crazy and Ugly.

After dessert, I headed back to my dressing room to get ready for bed. I stared at myself long and hard in the looking glass and did not like what I saw. Crazy and Ugly had obtained eternal youth, and Snow White would soon have her Prince. Eventually, I would have freedom from all of them. That's when I realized I hated all three for exactly the same reason - they were more beautiful than me!

I gasped at the grave error I had almost made.   I had the fairest maiden in all the land right at my fingertips.   If I ate her heart, I would possess her beauty forevermore and be done with her permanently!

I hadn't practiced witchcraft in years, but I couldn't possibly let an opportunity like this slip through my fingers.   I was so excited, I could barely sleep.   Thank heavens, Snow White did not agree to marry the Prince!

In the morning, I received word that the Prince and his men departed for home early.   He must have felt most unwelcome by Snow White's rejection of him over dinner.   I was so content, I happily sat in my sitting room eating strawberry tarts while contemplating how to bring about Snow White's death without linking it back to me.

Imagine my surprise when Snow White burst into the room, accused me of denying her sweets and all but dived at the platter of pastries.   My little lamb was showing glimpses of a lioness; it was all the more reason to be rid of her as soon as possible.   I pointed out her erratic behavior must have a reason, and she again insisted that she alone would choose her future mate.   She accused me of treating her like a child and when she asked to be given more responsibility as a Princess, a plan began to form in my mind.   I told her I would send for her later.

I returned to my bedchamber and opened my top dresser drawer. Back when I was angry about not having a baby, the royal physician prescribed a sleeping agent to aid my insomnia.   I still had a vial of it left. It wasn't poison, but if it knocked her out, the rest would come easily.   I put the vial in my pocket and then began to search my closet.   I knew I had it buried somewhere and at last I found it - the heart shaped wooden box. Though I had scrubbed it clean, it was still stained with human blood and smelled of death.

I made my way to the throne room and asked that the royal huntsman be sent for to speak with me privately.   When he arrived, the doors were shut tightly, and I got down to business.

"I have reason to suspect Princess Snow White of committing treason. Rather than endure the humiliation of a public execution, I would prefer this matter be settled in a quiet manner," I explained to the huntsman.

"You want me to assassinate the Princess?" he asked, startled.

I handed him the vial of sleeping potion.   "This will knock her out, the rest will be up to you.   I don't care in what manner you execute her; I only ask that you bring me back her heart as proof.   You may rest assured that her death will be presented to the kingdom as an accident."   I handed him the box as well, and he put both items into a saddlebag he was carrying.

"I expect there will be sizeable compensation for the job," he said with absolutely no remorse over what was expected of him.

"Keeping your job and your life should be its own reward," I smugly reminded him.

"I understand, Your Majesty," he said, now growing pale.   It must have finally occurred to him that if I had no qualms killing my own stepdaughter, his life was undeniably trivial to me.

I had a servant send for Snow White and explained to her that the huntsman would accompany her on a surveying expedition.   They were to determine exactly where our border met with Starlightdorf.   She was pleased with the new responsibility I had appointed to her and left willingly with the huntsman.

I sighed with relief when they had left.   I was content with how well my scheme was working.   I left the throne room and made my way to one of my parlors.   I set up a circle of candles on the table.   I didn't sit in this room often, because of the disturbing memories it held.   Now, all I had to do was wait.

I took a book off a nearby shelf to occupy my thoughts.   It was a translation of the Greek play, Medea.   When I opened the book, a piece of paper fell to the floor.   I picked it up and stared at the tarot card Crazy had painted.   It was the one with the woman eating an apple - the card that supposedly represented Snow White's future.   I tucked it back into the book as I hummed, "An apple a day, will keep her away."

Abnormally Attracted to Sin

"She may be dead to you, but her hips sway a natural kind of faith,

That could give your lost heart, a warm chapel." — Tori Amos

As it grew later, I decided to retire to my bed chamber.   I gave orders to be informed immediately when the huntsman returned.   I couldn't imagine what was taking so long.   How far into the wilderness had he taken her?

I crawled into bed and continued reading the play.   I must have drifted off to sleep at some point because I dreamed I was soaring through the sky on a chariot pulled by dragons.

I awoke in the morning feeling far less in control.   Had something gone wrong?   Did the huntsman take pity on Snow White and help her escape?   I hated the waiting and not knowing.   Even bad news was better than no news at all.

I tried to keep busy, but nothing seemed to distract me.   Time can be a strange thing.   Some days fly by in the blink of an eye while others last an absolute eternity.

It was nearly sunset when I received word that the huntsman had returned.   I had him meet me alone in my sitting room.   He arrived looking harried and appeared to be injured, for his clothes were stained with blood.   Still, he handed me the wooden box with a look of triumph.

"You look terrible," I pointed out the obvious.

"She put up quite a fight, but as you can see, she did not win," he responded.

"Then what on earth took so long?   I expected you back a day ago!" I said, fuming.

"She temporarily got away; I had to track her through the forest at night," he explained.

"So you didn't knock her out?"

"I tried to, but she had a strong spirit.   She saw through the ruse at once and managed to attack me as well!"

I couldn't imagine helpless Snow White committing an act of violence. I began to suspect that he was lying, though his story struck me as pathetic rather than heroic.

"I need to attend to my injury," he said as he headed for the door.

"You are not dismissed yet," I informed him.   I opened the heart shaped box and the putrid smell of death wafted into the room.   The organ inside looked familiar, but not at all what I was expecting.   "This is a boar's heart," I declared.

The huntsman was now sweating profusely.   "My Queen, I swear to you that it is the heart of Snow White, just as I promised."

I bit into the heart, chewed and swallowed.   With blood dripping from my mouth, I repeated, "This is not her heart; this is the heart of a boar!"

194

"How could you possibly know the difference?!" the huntsman began to sob.

"I eat young girls' hearts for breakfast - that's why!" I shouted at him. "No mere pig can abate my hunger!"

"Eating human flesh makes you a witch or a demon!" he sputtered with fear.

"Or worse!" I added. "So if you wish to avoid my wrath, you will tell me the truth!"

"Snow White tricked me and got away. I got severely slowed down when she stabbed me. I lost her trail and knew I couldn't return to you empty handed. So I captured a boar and cut out its heart." The incompetence spilled from his lips, and I was disgusted. "There's no way she can survive in the forest alone," he continued. "She'll die of starvation or be killed by a bear. She's so disoriented, she'll never find her way back even if she does live."

"I've heard enough!" I told him. "Of course, you are right. As long as she doesn't return, your mission was accomplished. Your accusations of me being a demon are, however, another matter."

"I was joking, Your Majesty!" he tried to assure me. "You saw through my lies, so I claimed you were bewitched. Obviously, that is not the case. You were simply being astute, observant and wise. I beg of you to forgive my outburst and have mercy on me!"

"Oh, how I hate to see a grown man grovel!" I sighed. "You may go!"

He couldn't leave my side quickly enough. Of course, I didn't trust him to remain silent.   I suppose eating a raw heart in view of anyone could be looked upon as upsetting.   But it was too late now, so I would just have to live, learn and move on.

I summoned two guards to me.   "The royal huntsman is to be arrested," I informed them.   "The Princess was lost in the woods while under his supervision.   She is now presumed dead.   For his negligence, he too shall die."

"Understood," they responded in unison before departing.

I slapped my hands together as if washing them of the matter.   I could always sacrifice another maiden for beauty's sake at another time.   In the meantime, I could content myself with the certainty that Snow White would not be coming back.

As the days passed, I continued to feel uneasy.   Without proof of her demise, I grew reluctant to believe that Snow White was actually dead.   If she managed to escape and was able to convince others of her royal bloodline, they might aid her in a rebellion to remove me from the throne. Paranoia was making me restless.   I soon realized I would have no peace until her body was discovered.

I sent a large regiment of men and hounds to search the forest for any traces of the lost Princess.   Nothing ever was found.   The news of Snow White missing spread throughout Whitebirchburg like a wildfire.   I had no idea how beloved she was by the people until she was gone.   Mass hysteria lead me to hold a memorial service in her honor, so that her death would be acknowledged and widely accepted.   The search parties were called off, and a celebration of her life took place at the palace.

And still, I could not let it go.   I was determined to discover something of her fate.   So, one morning, I woke up early and decided to take action. I made my way to the rose garden, which was empty, and arranged some stones in the shape of a circle.   Though I hadn't performed an animal enchantment in years, the words to the incantation fell from my lips as if I recited them everyday.

"To this circle, I summon thee,

To be my eyes and spy for me.

Birds with feathers black as night,

Show me the girl with skin snow white."

I placed my hands on the ground and a flock of ravens flew down and surrounded me.   Then with fingers interlocked, I lifted my arms to the sky, and as I parted my hands, the birds ascended and dispersed.   I knew if they found anything, they would return to me.   So, I filled the bird bath in the garden with water from the courtyard well and then returned inside the castle.

Throughout the day, I would glance outside to see if any of the birds had returned. They never did.   The weeks began to pass again.   Finally, even I was convinced that my stepdaughter was dead.

Life began to resume normally.   Each day, I grew older and whenever I saw myself in the looking glass, my beauty grew dimmer in the reflection. With Snow White removed from the equation, it was time to find a replacement maiden whose heart I could possess.   This time I would have to do the deed myself instead of relying on the ineptitude of others.   I wondered frequently who my victim should be and how to dispose of her body after devouring her heart.   It was a matter that would have to be handled very carefully.

I watched the young, pretty servants as they came and went.   I tried to determine which ones were still pure and who among them was the most beautiful.   And then she came into my life, as if a gift form the dark Gods. Her name was Gretah, and she belonged to a wealthy, aristocratic family. She first corresponded to me through a desperate letter.

Queen Lilith,

My name is Gretah Birchwood.   We have never met, but you have spent time in the company of my parents on occasion. My father is a successful merchant whose business has thrived under your leadership.

I hope you will not find it too forward of me to ask for your assistance in a personal matter that has caused a rift between my parents and me.   I know that they will listen to you, and I'm hoping that you might speak to them on my behalf.

When I was still a baby, my parents betrothed me to the son of a Baron.   He is a year older than I, he is handsome and polite, his family is very kind, and we all get along quite well.   The problem is that I do not wish to get married - not just to my fiancé, but to anyone at all.

I know that this sounds rather shocking, but please allow me to explain.   I am a very devout Christian, who was fortunate enough to be born into a wealthy family and afforded the opportunity to learn to read, write, and study the Bible and other theological works. Being greatly influenced by the writings of St. Paul, I began to see that the best way to assure eternity with our Heavenly Father is to remain pure in body.

Though my primary basis not to marry is religious, I have other reasons as well. I do not want to be considered the property of my father or my husband. I wish to be a woman in control of my own destiny. As a woman of power, who makes decisions independently, I thought you might relate to my plight.

I also do not appreciate that the role of women has been reduced to the single function of procreation. Being a mother is not equivalent with being a woman. I have many dreams in my heart, but raising children is not among them. Why should I be forced to do so simply because others think that it is only proper?

I hope, My Queen, that you might come to my aid. You exemplify strength and courage. Please help me convince my family that I, too, can lead a meaningful life without relying on a man.

Sincerely,

Gretah Birchwood

After reading her letter, I was filled with a mixture of emotions. She seemed intelligent, and I could relate to her wish for control of her life. At the same time, she was so very different from myself. I never grew up with a father making decisions for me. She also seemed to genuinely care about her fiancé so I could not understand her reasons why she refused to marry him. Her theological views were obviously not my own, and her reluctance to be a mother, I also found odd.   Remaining childfree by choice was nothing like being childless due to circumstances beyond your control. I sympathized with her, but hated her at the same time.   Mostly, I noticed from her letter what an easy mark she was.

I invited her to join me for dinner at the palace, but she was unable to comply because her own father had her arrested.   When word reached me, I made the journey into town to visit her in prison.   Her punishment for failing to marry had yet to be determined, so I rushed to settle the matter myself.

When I made my arrival, I saw her for the first time huddled in her cell with one arm chained to the stone wall.   She was no older than Snow White had been.   Her skin was smooth and creamy, and her hair was as pale as corn silk.   Most amazing were her eyes that shone a brilliant blue that looked liked the depths of the ocean.   Her cheeks were stained with tears, but it was undeniable how lovely she was.   She met all my requirements: young, chaste, beautiful and, perhaps most importantly, vulnerable.

"Gretah, I'm here to rescue you!" I announced to the distressed child.

She looked at me with eyes full of relief.   "My Queen, my prayers are now answered!   I knew you would come!"

Her presumptuous attitude irritated me.   "How did you know that I would come?"

"Because you could not save your stepdaughter," she replied. "Helping me will give you a much needed sense of atonement.   I prayed to

God for guidance and that was the answer he provided me." Her words put me in a stunned silence. "Am I wrong? Aren't you here because of Princess Snow White?"

"In fact, I am," I said, though the truth was not as she perceived it.

"I thought so," she smiled. "I know that my father has taken this measure to frighten me, but of course, he doesn't hate me. After all, it's impossible for a father to hate his daughter."

"I wouldn't be so sure about that," I had to disagree.

She ignored my comment and continued, "But I'm no longer scared, now that you are here. Coming here today is the beginning of something bigger than ourselves. You'll be responsible for emancipating the women of this kingdom from being the property of men!"

"That is not why I'm here," I corrected her. "I believe women already have the power to shape their own lives. I'm here today out of concern for your eternal soul."

"So, you do understand!" she said in relief.

"Absolutely," I said, as I held her hand that was free. "I wish you to arrive at the gates of heaven as pure as when you entered this world."

"Then you'll help free me?" she asked with anticipation.

"Of course!" I assured her.

"When?" she wondered eagerly.

"Right now!" I said as I slammed her against the stone wall and slit her throat with a dagger I was concealing in my dress. Blood began to pour from the wound as her blue eyes stared at me with betrayed bewilderment.

Her body hung limply from its chain.   I had made her wish come true, I decided proudly.   She died a martyr and would now be embraced in the afterlife.

I summoned the guards and ordered them to cut out her heart and bring it at once to me in the palace.   I explained that she was a heretic who needed to be made an example of for the sake of the kingdom.

I didn't wait around to watch her ribcage be broken as her heart was removed.   I didn't see her father arrive blaming himself for his sweet girl's fate.   I didn't witness her burial at her family's grave plot, or her fiancé crying for all that could have been.   Still, I could imagine all these details in my mind as I returned to the castle.

I took a warm bath and washed away the blood that had splattered my skin.   Though I'd been responsible for deaths before, this was the first time I caused the fatal blow.   Strangely, I felt calm rather than guilt ridden.   It was as if I had finally manifested into what I was truly capable of being. How odd that it would bring me so much satisfaction.

I emerged from the bath and wrapped myself in a silken robe.   I shut myself in the sitting room and made a fire.   The heart was waiting for me on the table.   It wasn't in the wooden box, but inside a bucket commonly used for collecting apples from the orchard.   I did not see Gretah's face as I looked at the lifeless organ.   It was now just a piece of meat.

I cooked it over the fire and then prepared to eat.   I lit a circle of candles and proclaimed:

"I sacrificed this maiden chaste,

So I could gain a younger face.

Beauty will mask my hidden truth,

And serve as my fountain of youth.

I drink this blood and eat this meat,

So that my spell will be complete."

Then I bit into the heart and swallowed. The texture was tough, but the taste was juicy. As strange as it seems, it was just as delicious as the boar's heart I had eaten all those years ago. I devoured it quickly, but didn't feel any differently. I began to doubt that the spell had worked. I sat in the room reading for a short while, daring not to look into the mirror.

At last, I headed to bed. As I got undressed, I inadvertently looked into the mirror and was shocked at what I saw. It was me, but younger and more radiant than I had ever looked! I seemed about the same age that Snow White was when she disappeared. No gray hair, no fine lines, no age spots - all of it had simply vanished. I was successful as a witch after all!

I was much too excited to sleep, and yet in the morning, I didn't look tired at all. I got dressed, painted my face and styled my hair as if I were playing with a life size doll. With my crown firmly in place, I headed to the throne room and went over the day's agenda.

Relations with Starlightdorf were still on the mend, and the King was sending his son to implement a new trade route through their territory that would benefit both lands. I hadn't seen the Prince since the death of Snow White. Considering how they last parted, I was fairly certain he wouldn't care too much about her fate.

That's when an idea entered my brain.   Now that I was looking gloriously young and gorgeous, why not seduce the handsome Prince myself?   How could he possibly refuse beauty as rare as mine?   I suddenly couldn't wait for the affairs of the day to commence.

The Space in Between

"Arms entwined in a final pose, narrative drawing to a close,

Still remain the things we couldn't kill, in your eyes I can see it still."

- Mariqueen Maandig

"With trade negotiations now firmly in place, I see no reason for any bad feelings to fester between our kingdoms," the young Prince stated as our meeting was drawing to a close.

"Agreed," I said with a reassuring smile. "Let us leave all hostility in the past and move forward with our united goals of peace and prosperity."

"My father will be most pleased to receive news of a resolution to our former disputes," replied the Prince.

"I hope you won't be leaving too soon!" I interjected. "We will be having a gala celebration in your honor this evening - dancing in the ballroom, a feast of venison and wild boar, bottles of vintage wine and fireworks at midnight!"

"You certainly know how to throw a party, Your Majesty," the Prince laughed. "I trust your fair Princess will be joining us this evening?"

"Oh dear, you haven't heard," I said suddenly somber. "Princess Snow White is no longer with us."

"What do you mean?" he asked, disappointed. "Did she marry and move away?"

"No, she became lost in the woods on an outing and never returned home. It's been several months and though we never found her body, we can only assume that she is dead," I explained.

"How could you possibly think of celebrating in the midst of your grieving?!" he asked with anger.

"It is because the kingdom has been in mourning that I am eager for some joyful news!" I defended myself. "Snow White's memorial service was held in the spring, and it is now autumn. I do not wish my people to be forlorn forever. Please try to understand my position!"

"I find it revolting and will have no part of it! I strongly suggest you cancel the festivities at once if you hope to maintain the truce with my kingdom," he sternly advised.

"Of course!" I relented. "I don't wish to do anything that will negate what we have worked so hard on these precious months."

"I wish to pay my respects to your stepdaughter before I leave," he continued.

"As I already mentioned, we never found her remains. Therefore, there is no grave to visit," I told him.

"You have no statue or stone marker as a memorial?" I shook my head. "Then may you take me to her room?"

"Her bedchamber has already been cleared of her things. It was too heartbreaking to have these reminders of her around me."

"I'm sorry to have intruded during such a sad time for you," the Prince apologized. "I think it's best if I now be on my way."

I grasped his hand tightly before he could walk away. Inspired to perform well, I began to cry. "Please don't go!" I begged him. "I've been so lonely for company since Snow White's death."

"I'm sorry for the many losses you have had to endure, but spending time with me will not heal your wounds," he said as he awkwardly backed away from me.

"I disagree," I said as I wrapped my arms around him in a desperate embrace. I pressed my breasts against him and whispered in his ear, "Any distraction would help me forget my hurt."

Yet despite my best efforts, the Prince pushed me away. "I'm sorry, fair Queen, but I feel I must resist any action that could lead to future regret on your part, as well as mine. Let us be glad for the progress we have made here today and look forward to a promising future. In the meantime, I pray for Snow White and those left behind who loved her." Then he walked away quickly, as if afraid to hear any more from me.

I fought the urge to chase after him. If I threw myself at him again, it would simply look pathetic. Unlike my late husband, the Prince was handsome and intelligent, and I wanted badly to make him mine. But now it seemed I would have to wait for a more opportune moment.

From the balcony overlooking the courtyard, I watched him assemble his men and order them to prepare their horses for departure. And then the Prince did something truly unexpected. He kneeled before the courtyard well and bowed his head in prayer.   Was he sending a final farewell to Snow White?   Did he refuse my advances because he had secretly loved the Princess?   My blood began to boil as I realized even in death, I could not compete with her.

I stared at the well long after the Prince had left.   Perhaps, I was imagining things.   After all, Snow White could never belong to him now. How absurd of me to be jealous of the deceased when I was not only alive, but more beautiful and powerful than I had ever been!

Suddenly, I saw a flash of black catch my eye.   A raven had appeared and made a descent into the rose garden.   My heart pounded in disbelief. I ran down the main staircase and outside the castle doors.   Surely this was just a random bird, who happened to appear while I was in an agitated state, but I had to make sure.   I raced into the rose garden and saw the black bird perched on the edge of the now empty bird bath.

I returned to the courtyard and drew a pail of water from the well.   As I did so, I felt the Prince's aura lingering there, judging me for disposing of the Princess.   My rational mind knew that there was no possible way the Prince could know of my involvement in her disappearance, but at the moment it was my irrational mind that was dominating my being.

I poured the water into the bird bath and said, "Water become a mirror to me, and reflect everything this bird did see."

The raven poked his beak into the bath, and in the surface of the water, I saw a vision of a cottage in the woods.   Snow White emerged from the door looking haggard, but still I could recognize her.   And then a group of little men also popped out of the house to join the Princess.   At first the shock of seeing my stepdaughter alive terrified me, but then as recognition set in, I realized I could still mend the situation.

"I know that house!" I announced to the raven, who tilted his head thoughtfully.   "I've been there before - it's the cottage of the seven dwarfs!"   I chuckled to myself as I began to formulate my new plan for eliminating my stepdaughter.   I no longer needed her heart, but I did need her dead to ensure she wouldn't turn the kingdom against me.   Still, something about her left me feeling unsettled though I couldn't quite put my finger on it.   The raven flew away before I could glimpse her reflection again, but I was certain of what I had seen.   Snow White was hiding in the forest, hoping I would never find her.

It took a few days for me to make the necessary preparations.   I would need a disguise, a distraction and a weapon.   Once everything was in order, I announced that I would be leaving on business but would return before a week had passed.   A few servants dared to inquire more details for security purposes, but a single glare from me made them abandon their interrogation.

I left the palace not a moment too soon.   Everywhere I looked I saw pieces of her - apple seeds spread upon a table, her tarot card marking my place in a favorite book, her song echoing in my head and her likeness appearing on the face of an ordinary servant girl.   I mounted my beautiful steed, Phillip, and galloped into the forest, following the same route I took with Ugly so many years ago.   I never guessed that I would ever return.

Phillip was the fastest horse in the kingdom, and I knew he would help me reach my destination as soon as possible, so that I could return just as quickly.

Once I was near the dwarfs' cottage, I searched through my saddlebag and changed into simple peasant clothing. I hadn't used my seamstress skills in years, but found that creating such an outfit took little time. I suppose some things are never forgotten even after a lack of practice. I wiped off my lip color and shook my hair out of its braid. Wavy locks now hung to my waist, but still I feared I'd be recognized.

"Because Snow White is not yet dead,

Let me change my hair to red."

I sprinkled a potion of rain water, poppy petals and three drops of my own blood into my hair, and it instantly transformed to a brilliant shade of scarlet. No one would ever mistake me for being the Queen now.

Phillip was tied to a tree, and I now made my way to the cottage. I knocked on the door, but there was no answer. Surely Snow White would not be foolish enough to open up to a stranger.

I tried the door handle and it opened easily. I wandered inside, but no one was there. At first, I thought Snow White might be hiding, but I opened every closet and looked under every bed to no avail. The little men had to be at work. The stench permeating from the dirty pots and pans indicated that the dwarfs had been doing the cooking. Had I imagined that Snow White had been here?

Then I noticed a purple embroidered dress folded up neatly with a tiara on top.   This was the very attire Snow White had been wearing the day she escaped the huntsman.   This was proof that she had been here.   But where could she have gone?   Surely she wasn't working in the mine with the dwarfs.   And if the dwarfs had been cooking for themselves, she must have left for more than the day.

I glanced at the gown again and remembered that she wasn't wearing it when the raven spotted her.   Yet there was something familiar about the dress with the blue bodice and golden skirt.   And then it hit me like a ton of bricks - I made that dress!   It was one of the princess gowns I designed when I was staying with Crazy and Ugly.   I took my favorite ones with me when I left to seduce the King.   A few were left behind, which could only mean that Snow White had been in contact with Crazy and Ugly and they had given her the dress.   Perhaps, she was, in fact, living with the witches. Maybe, like me, they were training her as a witch and she was only at the cottage for some sort of test like the one I'd been given.   It was possible that the witches wanted her to take revenge on me.   But then why was her dress and tiara still here with the dwarfs?

Clearly, I was confused over the details.   Yet, I did know that Crazy and Ugly were involved and this enraged me.   It was worse than anything else that I could fear!   The witches helped put me in power and were now helping my stepdaughter to become Queen instead.

I left the cottage and returned to Phillip.   Since I was already in disguise, I decided to ride to Crazy and Ugly's home and see for myself if Snow White was there.   The journey that took a day on foot in uncomfortable shoes, took no time at all on Phillip's back, my mind going over every possible scenario of what I would find when I arrived.

The homestead still appeared rickety, which surprised me. I would have guessed that with younger bodies, the witches would have made improvements to their living quarters. I knocked on the door, and Ugly answered. She looked at me with large eyes and shouted to her sister, "Well, kill a boar and sizzle some bacon - look who's here!"

Crazy came rushing over and said, "Piggy! It's been ages...what brings you to our neck of the woods?"

"How did you know it was me?" I asked incredulous as I ran my fingers through my red hair.

"You didn't do your eyebrows - such an amateur mistake!" Ugly pointed out.

"You look much younger as well," Crazy observed. "You must eat more than boar hearts these days."

"Enough with the small talk, ladies," I said getting straight to the point. "I've come here for Snow White."

"I haven't seen her since she was a child! What makes you think she'd be here?" asked Crazy.

"I saw a vision in which she was wearing a dress that I made and left here," I explained, still skeptical that they knew nothing.

"It's true; I saw here wearing the garment just the other day," Ugly informed her sister. "She must have stolen it that day we were robbed."

"You were robbed?" I asked in surprise. "How could such a thing happen?"

"We were out gathering herbs, and when we returned, we found some items missing - most of them food," Crazy shared.

"Our house is so frightful, it generally keeps trespassers away," Ugly added.

"Maybe she thought the house was abandoned when she was looking for shelter after she ran away," I took a guess.

"She ran away from home?" Crazy asked.

"Yes, but never mind that now.　Ugly, you saw her recently?"

"I did.　She was traveling with a dwarf, but shared no details of where they were going or why," Ugly revealed.　"She did however use the alias, Black Frost."

"She must be avoiding you if she's changed her name," Crazy decided.

"I think she's mounting an attack on me to remove me from the throne," I confided in the women.　"She needs to be stopped immediately!"

"What a nuisance!" Crazy sighed.　"This is why the two of us have never sought power...it's more trouble then it's worth!"

Ugly ignored her sister and announced, "Well, if we don't know where she's going, then your only choice is to bring her back here."

"How could I do that?" I asked, obviously missing something important.

"She's been living with the dwarfs and loves them like family... if anything were to happen to any one of them, I'm certain she'd drop everything and return," Ugly surmised.

"You think so?" I asked, not quite convinced.

"She's far more loyal than you," Crazy added in agreement.

"But if something happens to one of the dwarfs, how would they ever find out?" I wondered.

"The dwarfs have ways of communicating when they are apart; trust us, Piggy," Crazy assured me.

"But how will I know when she has returned?" I asked, still confused.

"Piggy, you worry too much," Crazy shook her head in disappointment.

"And you still don't think like a witch," Ugly scolded me. "I gave her my charm bracelet. It has a mirror that matches my sister's." Crazy held up her wrist to reveal a gold bracelet with a charm with a ruby on one side and a mirror on the other. "That mirror will be our window to Snow White's world."

I gave a sigh of relief. After all the drama among us, Crazy and Ugly were still going to help, and as usual, they were two steps ahead of me. Soon, Snow White would be dead, I would remain the Queen, and with time, the charming Prince would at last be mine.

Toxic

"With a taste of a poison paradise, I'm addicted to you,

Don't you know that you're toxic?"   - Britney Spears

Phillip carried me back to the dwarfs' cottage just in time for them to be arriving home from work.   My luck seemed even more remarkable as I found a single dwarf gathering berries from nearby bushes.   I only needed to harm one to bring Snow White back, and this one happened to be the easiest to deceive.   It was the same dwarf who gave me the gems back when I was training to be a witch.   I remembered that he didn't speak, but had a naïve nature that made this task all too easy to accomplish.

"Hello there, small friend," I greeted the dwarf.   "My horse is tired; would you mind if we rested a moment by your stream?"   The dwarf shook his head that he would not and motioned us to please relax.   I led Phillip to the cool water for a drink while I sat upon the bank.

The dwarf continued his business of picking berries and filling his basket.   After a short while, I rose and lead Phillip back to the little man. "Would you like to see a magick trick?" I asked him.   He gave me an inquisitive look, so I proceeded.   "This is an ordinary chicken egg, is it not?" I asked as I pulled the egg from my saddlebag.   The dwarf nodded.   "Put your hands out and see." He placed his hands with the palms up apprehensively as I cracked the egg. But instead of yolk, a gold coin fell from the shell and landed in his hands. His eyes grew large, and he looked at me with pure joy. "Don't get too excited," I laughed. "If that were real gold, I'd be a wealthy woman instead of a mere peasant passing through. The gold is only foil, but the chocolate inside it is real." He took the candy out of the foil and popped it in his mouth with delight. "Take care, friend!" I called to him as I mounted Phillip and rode away. The dwarf waved to me as I went, a smile gleaming on his innocent face.

"And now we wait!" I announced to the sisters as I returned to their home.

"Are you certain he ate the tainted sweet?" Ugly asked.

"I saw it with my own eyes," I replied.

"We used a much smaller dose of poison then we did on the King since a dwarf is tiny, and we don't want him to die immediately," Crazy said. "However, the task should be complete by the time Snow White arrives."

"I don't really care if he dies or not, so long as Snow White returns," I admitted. "Her death, on the other hand, must be swift to give my mind peace."

"Don't worry; we can come up with something unique for the precious Princess," Crazy assured me.

The following days were spent awaiting her return. I had imagined that spending time with Crazy and Ugly would be awkward, annoying, and full of tension. This, however, did not prove to be true. Being younger gave all of us a vibrance and light heartedness that didn't exist in our previous encounters.

I made each of them a new dress - a periwinkle one for Crazy to contrast her ginger hair and a sage one for Ugly to make her moss green eyes look even more intense.   I felt like my old self wielding needle and thread into something spectacular.

I left my life as Queen behind me for the moment and ran about barefooted with my hair undone and face unpainted.   We made a bonfire in the evening and danced about casting darkness upon the forest with our frolicking shadows.   In the morning, Ugly made a wreath of lavender for my hair, and Crazy cooked us omelettes made with mushrooms and onions.

Every once in awhile, Crazy would hold up her wrist and recite:

"Mirror, mirror, so very small,

My sister's mirror, I do call."

And the mirror would twinkle and show us an image of the view from Snow White's wrist.   The scenery went by in a blur; she must have acquired a horse.   At one point, she drew her hand through her ebony hair, and we caught a glimpse of her face.   There were tears in her eyes, which made the three of us howl with laughter.   I'm not sure why her pain gave me so much pleasure, but at least I was not alone in my opinion.

In the midst of this twisted camaraderie, it occurred to me that for the first time in my life, I had friends.   As Queen, I had no confidantes or aristocratic companions to whom I was close.   My mother had always been the person to who I felt the closest, and I never had girls my own age to play with while I was growing up.   Perhaps this was why my relationship with the sisters had mended itself.   We were all young in appearance now, making us feel more like peers.   I knew that in reality, they were far older than I, but they truly behaved as if they were younger.

"Do you miss it?" Ugly suddenly asked me.

"Miss what?" I questioned.

"Being carefree and unattached to any responsibility," she replied as if it was all too obvious.   "You pay a large price by playing Queen."

"I don't pretend to be the Queen; I am the Queen," I clarified.   "I feel that it is who I was always meant to be.   Still, it is nice to have a break. But what about the two of you?   What have you gained in being younger? You've not used beauty to become wealthy, powerful or even to seduce a man!"

"Eternal youth has granted us good health and the freedom to be true to ourselves," Ugly answered.   "Beauty can take us anywhere we choose, and in time, it will take us everywhere.   But for now, we are content just being ourselves."

"It seems a waste," I told her.   "But since we have nothing but time, to each her own."

Then Crazy ran into the room and announced, "She's back!   Take a look!"   So I held the charm on her bracelet and saw the faces of the weeping dwarfs.   "It's time to make the final preparations."

Ugly headed over to the shelves of dusty jars and bottles and grabbed a few in a selective manner.   "How about this one?" she asked her sister as she held out a small, red bottle with a cork stopper.

"Excellent choice," Crazy agreed. "This vial contains the venom of a poisonous viper found only in the African Congo."

"A descendant of the demon that invaded the Garden of Eden, so I'm told," Ugly informed me.

"Yes, it couldn't be more perfect!" I cackled with delight.

"The poison is instantly fatal. We just need something to tempt her with," Ugly sighed. "Another piece of chocolate, perhaps?"

"No!" I shouted with excitement. "I know just the thing...a red apple. It must be so irresistible that she can't possibly refuse it. Then just like her tarot card predicted, her fate will be sealed."

"Dearest Piggy, what a splendid idea!" Crazy declared. We had just been apple picking the day before, and I sorted through our bucket to find the one that looked the most delicious.

Ugly brought over a bowl and concocted a mixture made from a jar of water that was melted snow, crushed datura blossoms, the vial of poison, and a single drop of my own blood. Then I placed the apple in the midst of the solution to soak overnight.

"For the maiden fairest in the land,

Death by poisoned apple, I do command."

With the spell at work, I fell asleep. At dawn, I awoke eager to rid the world of Snow White.

"I was thinking last night that perhaps your disguise should make you look even more obscure, just to be sure your stepdaughter does not recognize you," Crazy suggested.

"What do you have in mind?" I asked.

"Why not approach her looking the opposite of what you really do? We could dress you as an old and homely hag."

"That would be extreme," I faltered, as I didn't wish to look ugly ever. Yet after a moment of thought, I decided it might not be a bad idea. "I could pretend to be a peddler; we could put together a basket of goods for me to sell. No one would ever be able to guess that I am actually the Queen!"

So with much excitement, I was fitted with a black, hooded cloak over my peasant garb. I cast the enchantment:

"Wrinkles, warts and sunken eyes,

Make for me my best disguise.

Age spots, limping and white hair,

Help me deliver this apple rare."

With my disguise now complete, I tucked the apple in my basket and had Phillip bring me back to the dwarfs' cottage. I watched and waited in the dense shrubbery, hoping an opportunity to be alone with my stepdaughter would present itself. Finally, she emerged from the cottage and began picking wild flowers. She was wearing the purple gown and tiara she had worn during our last encounter with each other. I left objects she might find interesting along a path leading further into the forest away from the dwarfs and their cottage.

Eventually, she glanced up, saw me and gave a jump. I'm not sure if she was startled to see someone standing there or more specifically by my frightening exterior.

"Come, child," I called to her. "I have fine wares for sale - pretty ribbons and combs for your hair."

"I'm sorry, but I'm in need of no such things," she stated.

"I didn't mean to frighten you, and will now be on my way," my crackly voice tried to reassure her. "I understand there is a house nearby, do you know if anyone there is home?"

"Please don't disturb us!" she begged me. "We've just had a death in our family." How quaint of her to regard these little men as family.

"My poor girl, I'm so very sorry for your loss," I lied. "Please forgive my intrusion and take this for your trouble." I pulled out the shiny, beautiful, red apple from my basket and offered it to her. "You know what they say about apples, child, don't you? Apples are for wishing. The redder the apple, the more likely your wish will come true," I tried to tempt her.

"No, I've not heard that before," she replied.

"Such silly nonsense, isn't it?" I sighed, as if not believing it myself. "Still, there's no harm in trying."

"This is the reddest apple I've ever seen," she said as she held it in her pale hands.

"An apple so pristine does look like it could be made of magick," I proclaimed.

"So what do I have to do?" she asked apprehensively.

"Just make a wish from your heart and take a bite," I stated.   I was making it all up as I went, but she now looked as if she were ready to believe.

"I wish that love was enough to bring the dead back to life."   Then she took a bite of the cursed apple.

A look of horror paralyzed her, and I worried that she would spit it out. "That is the magick working, dear child.   Now swallow, so your dream will come true."

Her throat moved and then her body collapsed to the ground.   The apple rolled from her hand and now remained at her side.   I watched her for several minutes to be sure that her breathing had stopped.   I laid my hand on her breast, but did not feel her heart beating.   At last, after so many restless nights, Snow White was finally dead!

"Beauty and youth to me restore,

Make me as I was before."

And at once, I looked like myself again.   I took the bracelet off my fallen stepdaughter and placed it in my saddlebag to return to Ugly.   I couldn't take her body back to the palace with me, so I decided to let the dwarfs dispose of it as they would.

I stopped at Crazy and Ugly's home to celebrate victory with wine and roasted goose.   We hugged, laughed, ate and were merry.   Finally, I changed back into my royal attire, had Crazy braid my hair, fixed the crown on my head and prepared Phillip for the journey home.

"Thank you, my friends," I called to the women.   "I've had more fun this week than ever before in my life.   Visit me at the palace anytime you wish!"

"Hail to the Queen!" they shouted as I left.   "Long may she live!"

I returned to the palace the following day to much fanfare.   I never did offer an explanation of where I had been, but I was in such good spirits that no one seemed to care.   I was genuinely happy to be home and sleeping in my own soft bed again.   As I undid my braid, my hair still smelled of lavender.

At long last, I had what I'd been seeking - power, beauty and peace. Much had been sacrificed along the way, but I paid the price to become Queen.   And yet, the memories of the past invaded my thoughts and threatened to haunt me.   A part of me wondered what my life could have been if only some critical choices were made differently.   Would that life be more worthwhile than the one I was now living?   I know it did no good to wonder about such matters, but I could not stop myself.   You can only bury a secret from yourself for so long before the denial overwhelms your soul.   And then you're left remembering all that was and all that could have been.

Bad Romance

"I want your love and I want your revenge,

you and me could write a bad romance."   - Lady Gaga

I explained my life "before" and "after" its biggest turning point.   The
year marked as "during" is one I like to suppress for my own sanity.   But
my story would not be whole without it, so every once in awhile I'm forced
to remember the sordid details.

At the age of twenty-three, I should have known better.   I wasn't a
child with a lack of good judgment.   However, I was inexperienced in the
ways of the world.   My life had been fairly sheltered - all I knew was my
mother, sewing and hard work.   I'd never had any adventure or romance in
my life so I miscalculated what I would risk for a taste of it.

One morning began like any other.   I headed to the bakery across
from our dress shop to buy some tarts for our breakfast.   There was a man
there that I hadn't seen before.   He was a bit older than me with rugged
good looks and a foreign looking attire.   He smiled at me, which made me
feel that he was friendly and approachable.

"Excuse me, Sir," I addressed him.   "That hat you're wearing...was it
made in England?"

"He seemed surprised. "Indeed it was. May I ask why you care?"

"Oh, I didn't mean to pry," I said embarrassed. "It's just that I'm quite interested in clothing. My mother is the royal seamstress for this kingdom, and I am her apprentice. We also have a shop across the way."

"Ah, what good fortune that we should meet! I'm a merchant and have been to England and France this past year. I have some amazing textiles that are not found anywhere around here. Would you like to take a look at them?" he offered.

"Of course, I would! Please stop by with them anytime today," I answered.

"Then I shall see you again soon, Miss," he smiled again.

"My name is Raven," I told him.

"So nice to meet you, Raven," he said. "Mine is Johann."

"Pleased to meet you as well," I gave a curtsey. "I'll see you later."

At the time, I was genuinely only thinking of the fabric. He had in his possession rare items, and I wanted them. I ran back to the shop to relate the entire encounter with my mother. She was far less excited than I, suspecting that this man intended to swindle us. Because of her immediate distrust, I found myself coming to his defense before he even arrived in our shop.

In the afternoon, he appeared with reams of fabric so beautiful I could not hide my eagerness in wanting to obtain many of them. There were so many different types of material and patterns that I became delirious with joy. Even my mother relented and decided we would purchase some of them if the price was fair.

An agreement was reached and though my mother was satisfied by the transaction, she was insulted that he helped himself to a strawberry tart without asking first.   I told her that a good hostess would have offered them, which she failed to do.   She maintained that he was rude, and the two of us did not speak to each other for the rest of the day.

I went to bed that night thinking about the various garments we would create.   It had been an exciting day all because I decided to speak to a stranger.

The next day, a bigger surprise awaited me when Johann arrived in our shop.   My mother was at the castle measuring some new servants and guards for their uniforms.   He seemed glad to see me alone.

"What brings you here today?" I asked warmly.

"I wanted to see if you could make me a new outfit," he smiled.   "I like to have clothes to reflect the various places I've visited."   I felt honored that he trusted my seamstress skills.

As I worked, he stayed and talked to me.   At first I was nervous, but his conversation put me at ease, as did that amazing smile of his.   The longer I looked at him, the more I realized how attractive I found him.   He had sandy blonde hair and hazel eyes.   He was strong, but laid back.   He made me laugh easily.   It wasn't until I was nearly done that I began to wonder if he had returned specifically to see me again.   I'd never had anyone flirt with me, so I immediately dismissed the idea.

When I had finished, I said, "Now you will have something to remember our kingdom."

"It's not Whitebirchburg I wish to remember," he informed me. "It's a memento of you." I blushed at the attention he was paying me. And then he leaned over and kissed me firmly on the lips as all my feelings of inadequacy melted away. I was immediately smitten by this gorgeous man who had the power to make me abandon my inhibitions. We kissed for a long while and then he spoke once more. "Tomorrow I leave to continue my travels. I wish there was a way that you could come with me."

"Must you go?" I asked as my heart pounded.

"I'm a merchant; I make my living through trade. I get to travel the world, but it is lonely at times," he confessed. "With you by my side, every day would be a fantastic adventure! We could eat delicious cuisine, learn new dances, see the sights of foreign lands and sail the seas."

He had me longing for things I had never even thought of before. Even though I had never wanted to travel or leave home, I suddenly felt its draw as if it were a need. I didn't see the danger of it. I didn't know that abandoning everything I knew in life would cost me dearly.

"I want to come with you!" I blurted out. He smiled coyly.

"I'll come pick you up at sunrise," he promised. One more kiss was placed upon my lips, and he was gone.

I started to pack my things. Objects I had recently cherished were now discarded as unnecessary as I went through everything I owned. I pulled out my favorite dresses and some ornaments for my hair. What was important was looking pretty enough to keep Johann interested in me.

I also began to pack a basket of food when my mother arrived home.

"What are you doing?" she asked with deep concern.

"I'm leaving home," I informed her.   "Johann asked me to be his travel companion, and I decided to accept."

"Have you lost your mind?!" she shouted.   "You don't even know him! I never raised you to be this foolish!"

"Precisely!" I replied.   "You never allowed me to have adventure in my life.   You never encouraged me to have dreams beyond our front door. I've never had such an opportunity before and will probably never have a chance like this ever again."

"You would choose a complete stranger over me?   I rely on you to help me with work," she pleaded.

"There are dozens of seamstresses in this kingdom to help you," I reminded her.

"But none as skilled as you!"

"You're just making excuses," I told her.

"Of course I am!   I don't want to lose you because of work, but because you're my daughter!   I love you more than any man ever could!" she cried out.

"I don't know if he loves me or not, but I love him!   If I let him leave, I'll regret it forever!" I informed her.

"What if you're wrong, Raven?" she proposed.   "What if instead you regret leaving?"

"I can always come back," I muttered.

"No," my mother stated.   "If you leave me for some man, your decision is made.   You can never return."

"Your hatred of men has made you mad!" I declared.   "Are you really forcing me to choose with such an ultimatum?"

"I am," she stood firm.

"Then I will choose the unknown and take my chance with Johann," I decided.

"I'm disappointed in you," she said.   Her anger or pride wouldn't allow her to cry in front of me.   These were the last words I ever heard from my mother.

"Perhaps one day you'll find it in your heart to forgive me," I said.   She remained stoic and silent and simply walked away.   I didn't know then that forgiveness would never be mine.

I couldn't really sleep that night.   I was too excited.   Well perhaps "excited" was not quite the right word.   I was nervous.   What if Johann changed his mind and left without me?   I didn't possess enough self worth to believe I could be desirable to a man.   But when morning arrived, he was there at the door with a smile gleaming brighter than the sun.

He had a large cart stacked with merchandise.   It was pulled by a pair of pure white horses.   To me, it looked like a dream carriage plucked out of my imagination.   Johann took my bags and placed them on the cart where they promptly vanished among his things.   We rode away as he held the reigns with one hand while his other hand was intertwined with mine.

Those first days together were a blissful dream.   Everything was new to me.   I didn't even keep track of the places we had traveled.   It was all a blur of sights, sound and color.   The world seemed bigger and brighter than I had ever thought it was.   It wasn't until much later that I would understand that the world held more promise in those days, not only because it was new, but because I was gazing at it through the eyes of love. With Johann beside me, anything seemed possible.   I could hardly believe that my mother chose to raise me with so much caution.   It was the happiest I had ever been.   I had no way of knowing how short lived it would be or how much deeper sadness is felt when followed by such intense joy.

We had made our way to the Mediterranean, and though I was so very far away from the only home I had ever known, I felt more myself here. This place had given birth to the western world as we now knew it, so maybe it made sense that my inner self was coming alive here as well.   I used my talents as a seamstress to make garments unlike anything the people of this region were used to seeing.   They sold for far more here than they ever would have at my mother's shop.   So for a time, we stopped traveling and set to the task of selling and trading.

"We'll sell off the things that were acquired on our way here and buy enough items of interest that we can profit from on our return journey," Johann explained to me.   "It's a continuous cycle that finances this lifestyle."

"If I didn't know any better," I chided him, "I'd think that you were keeping me around simply to make you money."   I laughed off such a crazy notion, but Johann remained silent.   Somehow, at the time I failed to notice, but my memory recalls it quite distinctly.

To wake up each morning and gaze at the sea filled my heart with quiet gladness.   I often sang to myself as if I were a siren luring others to me.   I forgot that sirens were harbingers of fierce destruction.   In retrospect, I realize it was a song of my own doom that I was invoking.

Growing up as I had, I saw marriage as an institution with no sacredness.   So although I was in love, I never burdened Johann with demands of such a commitment.   And when we made love to each other, it seemed like a celebration rather than a sin.

Given our location and the sheer bliss of our union, it's no wonder that Aphrodite decided to bless my womb.   My monthly bleeding had ceased and certain foods started tasting wrong.   I knew for sure I was expecting when smells became too intense and waves of nausea constantly washed over me.   Johann was initially convinced it was just food poisoning from eating too much shellfish.   Eventually, he realized I was the one who was correct.

His reaction to the news left little impression on me.   I assumed he was as happy as I was.   My mind immediately began to think in terms of being a mother.   Everyday, I would imagine my baby as a boy and then as a girl.   I saw an entire future of games we would play, lessons I would teach, meals I would prepare and songs we would sing.   I saw it all so clearly I would almost swear that it actually happened.   Yet, a life as wife and mother was a fantasy that would never come to pass.

After several weeks of motherhood daydreams, I noticed a spot of brown on my undergarments.   It had the look of old blood, but how was that possible?   My heart raced with panic.   Somehow I would will myself not to lose this pregnancy.   But the next day, I was spotting pink.   And then on the third day, it became a deep crimson red.   That's when I knew for certain that my baby had died.

I was unaccustomed to death and grief, so I remained inconsolable for many days.   The mental anguish of miscarriage was unrelenting, and yet it did not prepare me for the physical pain that would follow.   My abdomen felt as if it were constantly being stabbed with sharp daggers.   I could not walk or even stand; I just lied in bed, screaming in agony.   I bled and bled, and I knew that something had died inside me, because I felt like it might kill me as well.   After ten days of the most intense pain I had ever experienced, my body released all that was remaining of the brief life I had carried.   It was a horrifying experience.   I felt like I was living in a nightmare I couldn't wake up from no matter how hard I tried.

Such a loss played tricks on my mind.   I tried to rationalize why this had happened to me.   I wondered if I was being punished for being familiar with a man out of wedlock.   My brain wanted to make a bargain.   If God had taken my child, was it so Johann or my mother would not die instead? It was impossible to make sense of senselessness, but still I tried.

I did not want this to happen and could not believe that my own body had betrayed me.   It filled me with a deep sense of shame.   After I was well enough to walk again, I felt as if every stranger I passed by knew my

secret.   My irrational thoughts began to seem more plausible than facts.
I had been through circumstances beyond my control, and yet others must
have felt that I deserved it.   My biggest question was: Why?   I wondered -
Why me? Why this? Why now? - all day, everyday.

Johann kept busy with trade.   I did not see him much during those
days.   When we were together, he treated me as if I had lost my mind.
"You can have another baby someday," he insisted.

"I don't want another one!   I wanted this one!" I lamented.   "A baby
is not something that can be replaced."

"Why can't you acknowledge what you do have and just be happy?" he
responded.

"How can you say that?" I asked in shock.   "This was your child as
well!   Why are you not more upset?"

"This baby was more an idea than a reality to me," he confessed.   His
words broke my heart.   My life had changed.   I had been walking a path
that I was shoved off of suddenly.   His life remained the same as it had
been.   I was angry at him and jealous at the same time.

As usual, I cried myself to sleep.   The next morning, Johann informed
me that we were leaving to head back north.   It was fine by me.   The
romance of this region seemed to have disappeared.   Now when I looked
at the sea, all I saw was its cold depths and waves of loneliness.

I thought being on the road would bring us together once more, but
this did not prove to be true.   I didn't understand how the same tragedy
could rip us apart instead of bring us even closer.   And yet, I would not

permit failure into my life again.   I immersed myself in sewing and he in selling.   Still, the distraction of work did not alleviate my sorrow.

Even traveling through lands where no one knew me, I felt certain that everyone could look at my face and know the awful truth of what I'd been through.   I felt their gazes judging me as a defective woman.   Of course, this was all imagined, but its pain didn't feel any less real to me.

We were now in the kingdom north of Whitebirchburg.   I begged Johann not to take us on a route that would go any closer to home. Though I wanted to hug my mother now more than ever, I was too ashamed to face her.   I was sure she would tell me that she couldn't help me - that it was time for me to be an adult and figure this out on my own.

That night we slept at a local inn.   The fire was warm and the bed comfortable, but sleep came with difficulty.   Being near the vicinity of home, I felt the ghosts of my past drawing nearer.   But I know that eventually I did sleep because in the morning, I awoke alone.   Beside my clothes and shoes, there was some money and a letter.

Dearest Raven,

Our time together was brief and started out lovely, but I find myself unable to remain by your side.   I felt it was best to leave you near your homeland where you'll be able to make a living for yourself once more. You are no longer who you once were, and I'm sorry that I could not heal your hurt or share your sadness.   I sincerely hope the beautiful, talented woman I met will surface again someday, and you will find happiness.

Please do not attempt to follow me. The truth is I'm married and have two daughters in Spain. Your longing for family has shamed me into returning to them. I hope this gives you a chance to mend your relationship with your mother, for your sake as well as hers. I believe that everything happens for a reason. May time heal your heart and grant you a new perspective on life.

Johann

After reading the letter, I screamed and wailed like a wild animal. I'd experienced the deepest of sadness and now I felt anger beyond my capacity to handle. My soul was filled with pure rage. My mother had been correct after all! I couldn't return to her and admit how wrong I had been - my pride would not allow it. In truth, I was as stubborn as she. His philosophy on life happening as it should distressed me even more than the news of his secret family and my status as the other woman. I was meant to be a mother - I was certain of that! My baby was not supposed to die - to suggest otherwise was evil!

I eyed the pile of money left for me and counted it out. I was not properly compensated for all the garments I had made that he sold. I was merely a commodity to him in the end, and I finally saw all too clearly how that day in my mother's shop he had been auditioning me. And I played the role perfectly this past year, without ever realizing it! In the end, I had been betrayed, psychologically damaged, physically torn apart and financially duped.

I was so mad I could spit!   I wanted control over my life once and for all rather than trust that everything would turn out for the best in the end. Hatred was transforming me in wicked ways.   And thus, a plan began to form in my brain.   I felt like a victim who was now becoming a villain.

Oh, Father

"It's funny that way, you can get used to the tears and the pain,

What a child will believe, you never loved me."   – Madonna

I would not return to my mother as Johann suggested.   What I needed most at that moment was to take control of my life.   The first step as I saw it was to confront the person who caused hurt in my life right at the beginning.

I knew that my father lived in the kingdom where I was with his new family.   I'd never had any desire to meet him before, but now I felt like I had to for my own sanity.   I knew his name and that he raised cattle and sheep.   He met my mother when selling shearings to be processed into wool.   I asked the innkeeper where I might find him, after learning that Johann had settled the bill for our room before departing.   I was given exact directions from the innkeeper, who probably wanted me gone as quickly as possible or risk enduring another screaming tantrum.

Promptly, I was on my way.   It took the better part of the day to reach the homestead.   As I approached the door, I felt bold rather than nervous. I knocked and waited.   A man not much younger than myself appeared to let me in the doorway.   This was, I presumed, my half brother - my father's pride and joy.   He looked nothing like me.   His skin was olive and his hair was dark, but curly.   I wondered what his mother looked like.   I wanted to hate him, but some reason, I did not.

He smiled politely and greeted me, "Good morning, Miss!   How can I help someone as lovely as yourself?"

I was taken aback.   I was sure my eyes were red and my face puffy from crying.   Why was he being so kind to a stranger like me?   "Do you really think I'm beautiful?" I asked.

"Yes," he blushed.   "I'm Liam.   It's a pleasure to meet you, Miss." He extended his hand and shook mine.

"I'm Raven," I replied.   "Is your father at home?   He's the one I've come to see."

"Can I tell him what it's regarding?" he inquired.

"It's a personal matter," I told him.   "It pertains to my family."

He had me sit by the hearth while he went to find his father.   The home was cozy and beautifully decorated.   There was a hand carved cuckoo clock hanging on the wall.   It was intricately detailed, and I wondered if my father was talented and patient enough to have made it himself.

Soon, Liam reappeared with an older man.   His hands were rough and his features lined with wrinkles.   I was uncertain if he were older than my mother or if hard work had aged his face and body at a more rapid pace.

"What can I do for you, Miss?" he asked quizzically.

"Liam, if you could excuse us..." I prompted.

"Of course," he said.   "Hopefully, I'll see you later!"   He smiled again and walked away.

"Sir," I began, "I've come here for an explanation."

"To what?" his brow furrowed.

"To why I wasn't good enough for you," I said directly getting to the point.   "I'm your daughter, Raven, who you abandoned the day I was born."

He rubbed his temples and sighed with disgust.   "I never expected this day would come," he admitted.   "I figured a woman would not possess the courage to travel to a land unknown and face the man who did not want her.   Leave it to <u>her</u> to raise a daughter so brash!"   I did not appreciate the obvious contempt in his voice for my mother, though she never had kind words for him either.

"You may not have been prepared, but I am here nonetheless," I spoke.

"Very well," he sighed.   "Out with it then.   Tell me how wonderful your life was no thanks to me."

"Pardon me?" I said, taken aback.

"That is why you're here, is it not?   You're here to brag about what can be accomplished without a father's love.   Tell me all about the grandchildren I will never know, but I must warn you, I do not care."

I felt as if I'd been punched.   Here stood another man before me who did not care if my baby had lived or died.   My own disgust caused me to remark, "You think that's why I'm here?!   You couldn't be more wrong.   My life has been in shambles because I did not grow up with a male influence!"

"Ah, I see," he nodded as if now understanding. "You're here to put the blame on me rather than take responsibility for yourself."

"I did not come here to boast or place blame," I corrected him. "I was hoping for an apology, but didn't expect to get one. I came seeking only an explanation."

"You are right about not getting an apology," he stated. "I owe you nothing. So what is it that you wish to be explained?"

"I want to know why you left me," I said exasperated, as if it should be obvious. "How can any parent abandon their child?"

"Parents are human beings and, therefore, imperfect," he reminded me. "We're capable of being as selfish as anyone else. Girls giggle and cry too much, and worse of all, grow into women." I noticed that he hated women as much as my mother hated men.

"Men and women are not as different as you seem to believe. I feel badly for Liam, being influenced by your bias," I stated.

"What are you talking about? Liam's too soft. His sister remains his closest friend," my father grumbled.

"You have another daughter?!" I asked in shock.

"Violet is two years younger than Liam," he explained. "I was, of course, hoping for another son. Liam, however, loved her from the day she arrived. It made me love her too."

This confession was more than my already fragile state could bear. "You love my sister, though you could never love me." Saying the words out loud was a painful endeavor.   "Why?" I asked, desperate for a real answer.

He merely shrugged.   "It was a different time and situation from when you were born.   It doesn't change the fact that I despise women.   I don't like girls, but I do love Violet.   It is what it is."

"That explains nothing!" I retorted.   "Despite the fact that you love her, you remain firm in hating me!"

"True," he agreed.   "What use do I have for two daughters?"

"Every child is a blessing!" I informed him.   "How can you fail to see that?   After all this time, why are you not more enlightened?"

"You seem as if you are speaking from experience," he said with a haughty sneer.   "Are you now a mother?"

I bowed my head solemnly, trying to find the right words.   "I was going to be, but the baby died before it was born.   I wanted that child more than anything in the world, regardless of its gender.   I don't understand how any parent could feel otherwise."

"Really?   Then why is the baby's father not here at your side?"   His words hit me with the impact of a slap across the face.

"Death can test a relationship.   If birth was enough to chase you away from my mother, than you're in no position to judge what death can do!" I proclaimed.

"Make whatever excuses you want," he snorted.   "The truth is no man wants to be with a defective woman.   It seems, I, too, chose the correct daughter to support.   A woman who cannot bear a child is completely worthless to the world."

"Losing a baby is something that happened to me, it is not who I am! A single event cannot determine my value.   It is unfair to allow my self esteem to be dictated by a situation that was beyond my control!" Hearing this man decide that I was worthless made me finally realize for certain that I was not.

"Tell yourself what you must to carry on," he spoke sternly, "but in truth, you will always remain a failure as a woman."

"At least, I am not a failure as a human being as you are!"   I had had enough.   To continue a conversation with this horrible man was pointless. I stormed out of the house quickly, never looking back at the vile creature responsible for giving me life.

I decided to head back to town, but when I got to the edge of the field, I spotted Liam talking to a woman nearly his age.   "Violet, that's insane!" he said, and it caused me to freeze in my tracks.   This was her - the beloved daughter who had taken my place.   I walked slowly, at a pace that did not seem natural, but I wanted to overhear their conversation and try to make sense of what made this girl more special than me.

"I've already made up my mind, Liam," the olive skinned girl with dark ringlets and lavender dress spoke.   "Please be a good brother and be happy for me."

"You can't just run off with some merchant you've known for exactly one day and have me give my consent!" Liam attempted to talk sense to her.

"I believe in love at first sight!" Violet sighed. "He's the one I'm meant to be with; I can't let him leave without me!" As she blabbered on, I became infuriated. Johann was not returning to his family as promised, but already luring another maiden from her home. I suddenly felt incredibly stupid for falling for his charismatic smile as easily as I did. He had been a calculating creep all along, and my happiness with him had been nothing but a lie!

"What will you tell father?" Liam asked.

"Nothing," declared Violet. "I'll leave that to you. Frederick is picking me up in the morning, before the sun rises and the rooster announces the new day. I'll slip out without a word. I just can't bring myself to break Papa's heart!"

"So you'll make me do it?! That's not right!" Liam grew annoyed.

Again their conversation turned to drivel as I realized that Johann had never been his real name, as he was already using a new alias. Dangerous thoughts entered my mind, and I did not notice that I had stopped walking until I heard the click of the door as Violet went inside the house. Liam had spotted me and walked over to my side.

"Miss Raven, are you leaving so soon?" he asked with disappointment.

"Yes, my business here is done," I assured him.

"Might I convince you to stay for supper as my guest?" he asked with hopeful anticipation.

"That really wouldn't be appropriate," I turned him down.

"Please don't go!" he pleaded desperately. "What if I never see you again?"

"Then that will be as it should," I told him.   "Good-bye, Liam!"

"But Raven," he tried once more, "don't you believe in love at first sight?"

"No, I don't," I said as I thought of how Johann had used my vulnerabilities against me.   "This connection you feel with me is not romantic love; I am your half sister," I informed him.

"My sister?" he wondered as his face grew pale.   "Then why are you leaving?"

"Our father does not wish to acknowledge me," was my honest reply. I continued on my way.

"Come back!" Liam shouted.   "I cannot lose two sisters in one day!" But I did not turn back.   A new plan was forming in my head.

The details of what happened next are lost to me.   I remember hearing the story in town in the days that followed.   A merchant's cart had caught fire.   Trying to save what he could, the young man attempted to swat out the flames with a blanket.   But in the process, his clothes were set ablaze.   The young maiden accompanying him dashed to save him, but was swallowed by the flames as well.   The cart, goods, horses, merchant and maiden were all burned by the inferno.   The charred remains were beyond recognition.   No one knew the cause of the tragedy.

There were no rumors of a scorned lover sneaking onto the cart when he picked up the maiden or the incident being an act of arson, but I knew better.   I knew for sure that the man was Johann and the woman was my estranged sister, Violet, even though the remains could not be identified.   I could smell the acrid stench of flesh burning.   I could see the glow of the flames against the black sky, before the sun had risen.   Why did I remember these things if they were not part of the accounts I had heard?

I felt that they deserved their fate.   Johann had betrayed not just me, but a wife and two young daughters who like me were growing up without a father.   Violet was not so different from myself in the end.   Though our circumstances varied, our choice remained the same.   Life with a father and brother held a joy I did not know, but for a brief moment, at the end, she felt pain as I did.   And it consumed her whole.

I don't remember ever committing the crime, though I had a motive and no alibi I can recall.   It never seemed a part of my personal history.   It was just a story of something that had come to pass, not anything I have a memory of witnessing first hand.   But the brain has a way of protecting us by blocking out or changing details.   It has a way of convincing us of what we want to believe.

I just know that the news left me in a daze.   I didn't know where to go or what to do next.   So I made my way into the woods, as if disappearing from view was the only option that made some sense.   There I wandered until I met Crazy and Ugly.   And, well, you know the rest.

I killed my stepdaughter, so it stands to reason that I was capable of murdering the only man I ever loved and the sister I envied.   But did I really do it?   All I know for sure was that as I made my way into the forest, I whispered, "You died unexpectedly, Johann, but according to you, everything happens for a reason.   So I guess even you can agree that your demise was meant to be."

Start All Over

"Out of the fire and into the fire again, you make me want to forget and start all over."   - Miley Cyrus

Though phantoms of the past had been invading my thoughts, my general mood was one of merriment.   With the arrival of the winter solstice came two items that were unrelated, but both made a lasting impression on me.

The first was a box containing a pair of red silk shoes with dainty heels and decorative rosettes.   They looked bold and powerful and still delicate at the same time.   The note that accompanied the shoes read: *Only you know what it takes to walk a mile in your shoes*.   There was no signature, but I knew that it was a gift from Crazy and Ugly.   Only they would send something that looked both beautiful and dangerous.

The other item was an invitation to a wedding feast in Starlightdorf.   It seemed my handsome Prince had found himself a bride before I could complete my seduction of him.   At first, I was so insulted that I decided not to go.   Then curiosity got the better of me, and I realized I had to see for myself if the Prince's bride was more lovely than myself.   Plus, it was vital to maintain relations with their kingdom, so I decided I had little choice but to attend.

As the snow accumulated on the ground, I thought it a miserable time of year to have a wedding. I put on my ermine trimmed boots and heaviest fur cloak and proceeded to the carriage that would transport me to the celebration. It would be a long journey in the snow and even though I was bundled up, the cold air chilled me to my bones.

I began to regret my decision to attend this event. It was as if I had a premonition that something was going to go terribly wrong. The howling wind seemed to screech the guilt of my past sins. The more imperfect I was reminded I was, the more I longed to conceal my true self.

I brought along a magnificent ball gown of red satin and black trim. My newly acquired shoes matched the dress exactly. My goal was to make the young Prince jealous that he did not pick me to marry. But in truth, I was the one who was envious - of a woman I had never even met! It drove me mad that each time I felt a sense of peace, something new would occur to disrupt it.

That's when I decided I needed to arrive in disguise. The Prince had already rejected me, the Queen. Being myself was not good enough, so I would have to change my appearance to win his affection and steal him away from his fiancée.

I sorted through my overnight bag and pulled out a vial of liquid. I sprinkled the potion on my hair and recited:

"To make the Prince's heart grow fonder,

Turn my hair five shades blonder."

Instantly, my locks transformed into a golden hue.

The castle sat high upon a hill and when we arrived, I placed the hood of my cloak around me to conceal my hair. I flashed my invitation to the guards and was promptly escorted to my guest room within the palace. The weather had slowed my journey significantly, and I only had about an hour before the wedding ceremony began.

I quickly changed into my gown and painted my lips a matching red. I styled my blonde hair and slipped on my new shoes just as a knock was heard at my door. I opened the door and was surprised to see three royal guards as well as my coachman standing before me.

"Queen Lilith, I presume?" one of the guards inquired.

"No, you must be mistaken," I informed him.

They looked at the coachman for confirmation. "It's true...she is not my Queen."

"Is there anything I can help you with?" I asked with concern.

"We have orders to arrest the bride's stepmother for attempted murder," one of the guards revealed. "She was supposed to be brought to this room."

"Let me assure you, this is a case of mistaken identity," I notified them. "I am Lady Opal Fairmont, and I am much too young to be anyone's stepmother. I don't know what the woman you are searching for looks like, but I wish you luck. It would be such a shame to have this blessed day disrupted! Now, if you'll excuse me, I don't wish to be late to the ceremony."

My argument must have been convincing, but still the guards looked at the coachman. "I swear to you, Queen Lilith has dark hair. She is very beautiful, but looks nothing like this maiden," he explained.

"Forgive our intrusion," one of them spoke as they let me pass. There was chaotic chatter as I left. The guards were clearly worried about their breach of security.

Meanwhile, I strolled away serenely, though on the inside I was fuming. If I had not planned ahead and disguised myself, I'd be sitting in the dungeon at this very moment! My heart had dropped when they spoke the word "stepmother", and I began to wonder if by some miracle Snow White had been revived.

I hurried to find a seat for the ceremony. I no longer had time to intercept the Prince, but right now I didn't care. My mind was already plotting my escape since my coachman had turned against me. I would have to steal a horse and make the journey back by myself. But first, I needed to see the bride.

The guests were seated in rows in an oblong hallway that opened onto a terrace. The open doors exposed us to the frigid air that formed goose bumps upon my skin. The Prince stood on the balcony anxiously awaiting his bride. He looked so stupid in love that I wanted to leap from my chair and strangle the contented grin off his face.

Some string instruments played an arrangement of "Ave Maria" as the groom's parents were ushered to their seats. At last, the bride made her grand entrance down the aisle. All I could see was a blur of white lace as the guests all rose from their seats to admire the young Princess.   And then as she passed my row, I saw her face and had to suppress myself from releasing a scream.   The veil could not conceal the white skin, ebony hair and red lips.   There was no doubt that this was Snow White.

I managed to contain my anger and disgust for the duration of the ceremony.   I applauded politely with the other guests.   I made my way to the reception afterwards and downed a fifth of brandy followed by several glasses of champagne.   Although I knew I needed to remain alert, I worried that my tongue would become a vicious weapon if I were to stay sober. The only way to maintain the charade was to drink, laugh and dance.

I wasn't trying to draw attention to myself, but the red dress made it difficult for me to keep a low profile.   So I danced and flirted with the men brave enough to speak to me while I tried to plot my next move.

With Snow White alive and well, I knew that I could not return to my palace.   I'd be arrested and killed for being a fraud.   The truth I worked so hard to conceal was now rapidly becoming unraveled.   I had to flee, and the only place that came to mind was Crazy and Ugly's homestead.   But first, I wanted to get my revenge on the bride and groom.

There were white candles all around the room to add a warm ambiance.   I arranged some tapers so they would encircle the exquisite wedding cake.   I had no poison on me.   I could not kill the blushing bride, but I could curse her with lifelong misfortune.   I took the carving knife beside the cake and pricked my finger.   The white cake was covered with a design of butter cream snowdrops.   I let my blood drip on the flowers as I recited:

    "A witch's curse I place on thee,

    Let all who eat this live unhap-"

    But the incantation was interrupted by a man who grabbed my arm and said, "What are you doing? You can't put candlesticks on this table; they'll melt the cake!" At once he set to work moving them. There was something familiar about him, but I couldn't figure out what it was.

    "Why do you care?" I asked him. "You're not a servant. The cake arrangement is no business of yours." With my curse left incomplete, the mark upon my thigh began to throb.

    "Nor is it a matter that concerns you," he retorted. "Let us both step away and share a dance instead."

    "Very well," I relented, annoyed to have my plans fall apart once more. Nothing was going according to my wishes, and my frustration was nearly overwhelming.

    The gentleman placed his hand on the small of my back, and we began to waltz and glide across the ballroom floor. "Forgive my rudeness, but have we met before?" he asked me.

    "I don't believe so," I replied.

    "There's something familiar about you..." he insisted. He stared off into space as if trying to remember where he could have seen me before tonight. It made me uneasy because I felt the same sensation, and I didn't want him to recognize me as Queen Lilith.

    "How do you know the bride and groom?" I inquired, trying to change the subject.

"In a way, I'm the one who brought them together," he said beaming with pride.

"Whatever do you mean?" I asked.

"Princess Snowdrop was fleeing her kingdom, but before she could reach her Prince, she got word that a friend was in trouble. So, she had me deliver a letter to the Prince telling him where he could find her," he explained. "Without my help, they never would have reunited."

The rage that filled my soul had now reached its boiling point. As he spun me, I swung back around to the cake table and grabbed the carving knife. I twirled back in and held the knife to his throat. "This is all your fault!" I told him. But before I could pierce the knife into his flesh, I felt a severe pain that crippled me to the point that I lost my balance. It was my feet - they felt as if they were on fire. I fell into the arms of the man I had just tried to slaughter, and the knife fell to the floor with a clanking sound.

"Are you okay?" he asked me. I didn't understand how he could be worried about me when I had just attacked him.

"No, my feet are burning!" I whimpered in pain.

"Let's go outside to the terrace," he suggested.

"I'm not sure I can walk," I told him.

"Just lean on me," he instructed. I did, but each step I took felt like a dagger bearing into my foot. When we reached the balcony, we sat on a stone bench. "You must have squeezed your feet into shoes that were too small."

"They are new shoes, but they fit perfectly when I tried them on," I insisted. "Please, help me get them off!" I howled in pain, but the shoes would not budge no matter how hard he tugged. Though I was no longer putting weight on my feet, still the burning sensation continued. I was in such agony that tears flowed freely from my eyes.

As I glanced at my companion, his jaw was hanging open in disbelief. "Your hair...," he said. "It just changed color before my eyes." I held a lock of hair out and saw that it was now its natural dark color. It was as if the magick was being drained from my body. I raised my skirt up as my companion averted his eyes in embarrassment and saw that the witch's mark had disappeared! The scar that bore into my flesh all these years was now healed and smooth. And still my feet burned as if the shoes had been made of red hot iron.

As the man beside me looked at me again, he said, "I know you now! You're my sister, Raven!"

"Liam?" I asked as recognition finally took shape. He had the same olive skin and dark hair I remembered, but he looked so much older for I hadn't seen him in more than a decade.

"Yes, it's me!" he declared.

"Liam, please help me!" I begged him.

"I couldn't save Violet, but now I have been given a second chance," he said. "Raven, I promise to help you!"

At this point, my feet were black and bloody stumps that fell out of the red shoes. The smell of burnt flesh made my stomach revolt. Liam retreated inside and returned with a pitcher of water and several cloth napkins.   The pain was excruciating as he washed my wounds and bound them in the napkins.

"I must find you a physician at once!" he stated, but I grabbed his arm and shook my head "no".

"I'm not an invited guest here," I told him.   "If I'm discovered, I'll be arrested.   Now that my wig fell over the terrace, I risk being recognized."

"A wig?" he asked.   "But I thought I saw…"

"Please, brother - focus!" I redirected his attention.   "You must hide me; I have nowhere else to go!"

Instead of questioning why I was there, why I was in disguise, why I had tried to slice his throat with a cake knife and where I had come from, he simply nodded in agreement.   He had me place my arms around his shoulders and carried me through the ball room, down the main staircase and finally to the royal stable.   I hid my face and feigned drunkenness so nothing would appear unusual.   At last, we were on Liam's horse headed out in the snowy evening.

"Do you still live with our father?" I asked, now with new concerns invading my thoughts.

He sighed and said, "No.   Father committed suicide after our sister, Violet, died."   The pain in my feet made me flinch to imagine what Violet must have felt to be burned alive.   I also thought it ironic that my mother and father were more alike than different.   Both were proud and stubborn, and yet neither could cope with grief.   They both cowardly took their own lives.

"Do you have a wife and children?" I dared to ask next.

"No, I live alone," he responded. "I guess my upbringing caused me to have unresolved issues with women."

"Will you be unhappy to have me in your home?" I asked hesitantly.

"No," he said again. "I want you to stay with me."

"Good," I repeated, "because I have nowhere else to go." The pain of my wounds made me pass out before we ever reached Liam's home.

In the morning, I awoke to a doctor examining my injuries. In plain clothing and out of context, I supposed there was no danger of me being exposed as a Queen. My feet had to be amputated, and as I lied in bed I contemplated the fact that I would never walk again.

After the operation, I was in a state of delirium. It was at this point that I began to reexamine my relationship with Crazy and Ugly. I had no doubt that they gave me the shoes, so why did they choose to cripple me and take away my power as a witch? Were they threatened by me? Did they think it would slow me down enough to be captured and pay for my crimes? Were they responsible for reviving Snow White? Were we never friends at all?

And as I dropped in and out of consciousness, I thought of the bracelets with the mirror charms. They were linked, but they were not identical. Crazy's was embedded with a red stone, and Ugly's was engraved with a tree design. Suddenly, all too clearly, I understood. Crazy and Ugly were really Ruby and Willow. They were getting their vengeance on me for killing their mortal bodies even though their souls were reborn to Crazy and Ugly when they ate their hearts. They must have retained the memories of Crazy and Ugly and pretended to be my friend so I would not expect them to turn against me. I was relieved that I never told them anything of my past and true identity. At least I could rest easier knowing that they could never find me now.

I hid my past from Liam as well. There was no way he would ever suspect that I was the missing Queen from Whitebirchburg. Everyone spoke of Queen Lilith as a murderer and an evil witch. No one remembered the peace and prosperity I had brought to the land. Being human means having your flaws magnified and your accomplishments diminished. It made me glad to no longer be in the public eye.

The strangest part of the shift in power was that it was Gretah's fiancé who was appointed the new King. If I had not taken her heart, she may have relented in marrying him and lived to be the Queen herself. Instead, he married a young Princess with caramel colored hair and moss green eyes. Princess Willow's incessant sarcasm was so different from the pure and virtuous demeanor of Gretah that I imagined the King must be a pretty miserable man. Plus, he had her opinionated sister, Ruby, to contend with as well. I had thought they had no interest in palace living, but the royal headaches were theirs now, not mine.

Meanwhile, I was hiding in plain sight. I'm certain Snow White would be flabbergasted to learn that I was living within the realm of her new kingdom. But she didn't need to fear me now. My days of magick, curses

and murder had come to an end.   To stay alive, I needed to remain
undetected.

I could no longer walk, but when I was riding the many horses on our
property, I did not feel disabled.   Furthermore, our existence was more
than meager.   The Prince sent an annual sum of reward money to Liam for
delivering Snow White's letter.   Plus, I had started sewing again.   It
reminded me that more than a Queen or wife or stepmother, I was an artist
with fabric and thread.

At first, I found it odd to be living in the house where my father once
dwelled.   Every fiber of his being did not want me here, but perhaps that's
why I felt so smug to stay.   In the end, I took his place in the house while
he rotted six feet under.   Conquering someone who wronged me still made
me giddy.

Liam was kind and wonderful and seemed to overlook my many
shortcomings.   He never asked questions about the night of the Prince's
wedding.   I think he knew that he didn't want to know the truth about me.
It was an arrangement that worked quite well for us.   His denial of the
truth mingled well with my lies.   I'm certain that he often wondered why
my face and body never aged, but at last we both had family - why ruin it
with details of a past that was best left forgotten?

So, I buried my secrets like I always did and assumed this new identity
as sister...until you arrived.   You made me remember it all as if it had just
taken place.   The day your box appeared on our doorstep, I wondered how
you had found your way to me.   Your ornate filigree frame and reflective

surface echoed the past in my ageless face.   Did Ruby and Willow send you as a warning that they would always know where I am?   I feel too old to move on again, though my body remains eternally young.   So, I'll stay here with you and take my chances.

As I gaze at myself in your reflection, I think about who I was, who I hoped to be and who I became.   There were many things I desired - having a child, having the love of a lifelong companion, being asked for forgiveness from my repentant father, and having my mother forgive me for leaving her. But I was denied these things.   To endure grief, disappointment and depression and find your way back to yourself is no easy task.   I guess I did lose myself along the way.   Instead of facing reality, I transformed into a witch and a queen.   I refused to let life's failures hold me back.   Anyone who says they live a life of no regrets is either lying or has lead an extremely boring life.   I don't deny that I've made mistakes along the way.   But I don't seek redemption for my wrongdoings.   I just want the world to forget about me, so I can live out my days quietly for a change.   Though I have an immortal body, I'm not arrogant enough to believe that I will live forever.   Someday, someone will cut out my heart as well.

Now, you know the lies and the truth.   Well, not the whole truth. My real name isn't Raven.   Names are inconsequential after all.   Now when I stare at you, or rather stare at myself, I can smile now.   I'm not a mother.   I'm no longer Queen.   I don't have as much control over my life as I'd like to believe I do.   But I am a survivor.   I am me.   I am a woman with a secret or two left, and I wouldn't have it any other way.

ABOUT THE AUTHOR

Katie White is an author and artist, who graduated from Castleton State College in Vermont.   Her artwork consists mostly of watercolor and pastel drawings, as well as collages and comics.   After many years of writing short stories and essays, this is her first novel.   She currently resides in Claremont, NH with her husband and their many wonderful pets.

Made in the USA
Charleston, SC
07 October 2011